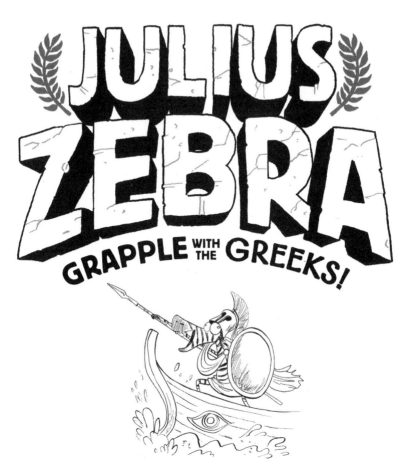

GARY NORTHFIELD

CANDLEWICK PRESS

For Arthur and Elsie: welcome to a
world of boneheads, nincompoops, and
holibobs. And that's before you start
reading these books! Love, Daddy

Thank you as always to Lizzie and Chloé.
Sorry for all the extra gray hairs.

Copyright © 2018 by Gary Northfield

First US edition 2021
First published by Walker Books Ltd. (UK) 2018

Library of Congress Catalog Card Number 2021935028
ISBN 978-1-5362-1514-4

21 22 23 24 25 26 LBM 10 9 8 7 6 5 4 3 2 1

Printed in Melrose Park, IL, USA

This book was typeset in Stempel Schneidler.

Candlewick Press
99 Dover Street
Somerville, Massachusetts 02144

www.candlewick.com

CONTENTS

So, you think you know about

JULIUS ZEBRA?

I know all there is to know!

Our handsome hero!

Julius wasn't like any other zebra and wasn't going to put up with this stranger's nonsense!

Exciting, right?

CHAPTER ONE

ADVENTURE TIME!

"Hey!" Julius cried at the stranger. "You can't just go around chucking my friends through the air!"

WHO DO YOU THINK YOU ARE?!

"I told you!" The muscle-bound man laughed. "I am HERACLES, son of ZEUS, and I seek the champion named JULIUS ZEBRA and his friends for an exciting adventure!"

"Listen, Hairy Knees, son of Zoots," retorted Julius.

"Heracles!" Heracles said moodily.

"That's what I said," continued Julius. "I'm not looking for any more adventures!"

1

Heracles seemed taken aback, and he bent over to have a good look at Julius. A big grin crept across his face, and he gave a huge belly laugh.

"YOU?" he exclaimed scornfully, and he took another close look at Julius, prodding him in his tummy and examining Julius's scrawny limbs.

Heracles suddenly felt a kick. He spun around and found a crocodile looking at him angrily.

"You take that back, you big bully!" Lucia fumed. "Julius IS a champion, so you'd BETTER say sorry! I don't care WHO you are!"

Heracles laughed again. "Ha, ha, ha! What odd, spirited creatures you are!" He gazed closely at the strange menagerie that stood before him. He grabbed Felix and held him in a headlock.

"And YOU, antelope, are YOU a great champion?"

Heracles let poor Felix drop to the ground as he paraded up and down in front of the animals, chuckling to himself.

"As you are no doubt aware," he boomed, "due to my vast legendary status, spanning the centuries and traversing all the known lands, I was tasked to complete twelve arduous labors."

"But it appears I was DECEIVED!" continued Heracles. "And one of my labors has since been UNDONE!" The demigod waved his arms defiantly toward the skies. "My father and ruler of all the gods, ZEUS, demands that I finally complete this labor if I am to take my place on Mount Olympus."

He turned directly to the animals. "I seek great champions to aid me on this quest, yet all I find are puny beasts CLAIMING to be the heroes of legend!"

He placed his giant hands on his hips in a dramatic pose. "So you leave me with little choice. You must PROVE your greatness to me!"

IV

Cornelius had heard enough. "We don't have to prove ANYTHING to you!" squeaked the little warthog, wagging his hoof. "In fact, how do we know YOU are who you say you are, huh?"

Heracles strode toward a rocky outcrop where two gnus stood minding their own business. He crouched and threw his big arms around the boulder.

"If you have heard of me," Heracles declared, "then you know I am the STRONGEST BEING that has EVER lived!" Then, with a great roar, he began LIFTING the enormous rock in the air, his face going a deep red as the veins in his forehead looked ready to pop.

A ripple of applause rose from the entranced animals.

"Bravo!" cried Felix. "I'm TOTALLY convinced!"

Heracles performed a small bow before hurling the boulder, with the gnus on top, toward the lake.

Julius was furious. "Can you PLEASE stop chucking animals around?" he yelled.

Heracles laughed as he flexed his muscles. "Calm down, Zebra. Have I not just proven that I am indeed the mightiest in all the lands?"

He placed a dusty hand on Julius's shoulder. "And now, you must prove who YOU are!"

"WE TOLD YOU!" Cornelius cried, still unimpressed. "We're not looking for any more adventures, so BUZZ OFF!"

"Yeah!" agreed Julius. "Why should we listen to you, anyway? What's in it for us?"

Heracles let out another of his deep guffaws. "What's in it for YOU?"

Those who help complete my final labor shall be granted IMMORTALITY!

"IMMORTALITY?" parroted Julius. "We don't need your immortality, sunshine! Now beat it!"

Julius turned to Cornelius. "What's immortality?" he whispered.

"Immortality is where you get to live forever and ever," replied Cornelius. "A bit like a god."

Julius raised an eyebrow. "So what, you don't die?"

"Not usually," said Cornelius.

Julius ran after Heracles, who had begun slowly striding away. "WAIT!" he called out. "We'll do it! We'll prove our greatness!"

Heracles turned around with a smug smile. "Excellent!" he proclaimed. "Already you show wisdom beyond your years!"

"What's Julius doing?" cried Lucia, perplexed. "I thought we'd told that big buffoon to get lost!"

Cornelius held his head in his hooves. "Yes, but now that Heracles has promised us all immortality, Julius has had a change of heart!"

Brutus poked his nose into the conversation. "Immortality?" He sniffed. "What's that in English?"

"Like I just told Julius, it's when you get to live forever, like a god," said Cornelius, holding his snout. "Hey, I thought your mom told you to get rid of that stinky seaweed wig!"

"Nothing comes between a zebra and his wig!" replied Brutus, brushing the seaweed gently with his hoof. "But forget all that—did you say we can be GODS? NOW you're speaking my language!"

As Cornelius buried his face once again in his hooves, a familiar figure approached the group.

"You're ALIVE!" cried Cornelius.

"Yes," growled Milus, brushing dust off his fur, "I'm alive." He gestured at Julius and Brutus. "Why are those IDIOTS talking to that lunatic?"

"We're all going to be GODS!" Felix piped up. "That big guy just promised us!"

Milus flopped backward into the rough sand.

CHAPTER TWO
OLYMPIC GOLD MUDDLE

Hunched over, Julius placed his front hooves on the line scratched in the dirt. He bent his back legs, poised like a coiled spring ready to leap into action at a moment's notice.

"ON YOUR MARK!" boomed Heracles, who stood to one side with his arm raised in the air. "GET SET . . ."

"GET OUT OF THE WAY!" cried Rufus as his long legs carried him through the melee and into the lead.

"That's really not fair!" huffed Cornelius as he scuttled behind, desperately trying to keep up. "I've only got little legs!"

Suddenly the warthog felt something hard land on his head and was shocked to find Brutus clomping over him like a stepping-stone!

But, as Brutus went to leap off Lucia's head, a great tug on his tail yanked him out of the air and hard onto the dusty earth.

As the barging animals scrambled around the lake, Julius steeled himself with a deep breath and charged ahead with a great roar of determination. Julius was DESPERATE to prove to Heracles that he was the legendary champion of Rome, worthy of his quest, and there was NO way he was going to let these idiots beat him!

Heracles sighed in solemn disappointment at the big tangle of arguing animals at his feet.

"You cannot be the celebrated heroes whose names echo around the Roman Empire," he said, tutting and shaking his head.

"Well, except me, of course!" announced Julius brightly, dusting himself down. "I'm a straight-up legend."

Heracles studied Julius quietly for a moment. "You are probably the MOST ridiculous!" he declared.

"Well, how rude!" protested Julius, frowning.

Not ONE of you has yet proven to me that you are worthy of my new QUEST!

Julius let out a big gasp. "But I'm Julius Zebra!" he cried. "Champion of Rome, savior of Britannia, liberator of enslaved beasts, AND former pharaoh of Egypt!"

Quest is my middle name!

Milus growled. "If your name gets any longer, Donkey, I'm definitely going to have to eat you."

Unconvinced, Heracles strode to the edge of the lake. "Follow me!" he declared.

He thrust his hands into the water and pulled out a large, flat, smooth stone. Standing at the edge with his back to the lake, Heracles swung the heavy stone in his outstretched right hand across his chest. He then quickly and dramatically spun around three times before loosing the stone across the entire expanse of water.

Heracles turned to Julius and the others. "You lot next!" he commanded. "Hit that tree and I'll know for a FACT that you're worthy of helping me complete my labor!"

"That's ridiculous!" blurted Felix. "That's MILES away! We'll NEVER hit it from here!"

"This just gets stupider and stupider!" huffed Brutus, folding his arms in indignation.

"If you do not hit it, then you will have failed and I, in turn, will also have failed," said Heracles. "You will NOT be the bold adventurers I have been seeking."

Julius stepped forward and walked to the water's edge. "Watch THIS!" he said.

After a quick scrabble around in the murky water, Julius pulled out a suitable stone.

Julius stood with his back to the lake and held out the stone in front of him, just as Heracles had done.

Then, desperately trying to remember the next moves, he spun his arms like windmills and threw himself into full-body rotation, twirling around and around, his arms outstretched like a spinning top. With a great gurgling grunt, he launched the stone high into the air.

Backward.

The whole lakeside erupted into laughter.

"Nice work, legend!" Milus snickered.

Cornelius ran up to his friend and patted him on the back. "Don't listen to them, Julius," he said. "I'd like to see them get it right the first time! Why don't you go next, Felix?"

"NO WAY!" spluttered the antelope, clutching a new rock he'd just found. "I collect rocks, not throw them away!"

Suddenly Rufus strode up, carrying Julius's stone. "Make way!" he said confidently. "I'll show you how it's done!"

I saw this drawn on the side of a jug in Rome!

Rufus held the pose for about ten seconds before everyone started to get restless.

"Throw it, then!" Brutus laughed. "I thought you said you saw it on a jug."

Rufus's face grew bright red with embarrassment, and he started sweating. "Yeah, well, they didn't show the next step."

"But you just watched Heracles!" Lucia reasoned. "Just copy him!"

Heracles buried his face in the palms of his hands. "We are doomed," he moaned. "Totally lost . . ."

"Give me that stone," growled Milus, snatching it from Rufus. The straggly maned lion flipped the discus-shaped stone into the air and deftly caught it behind his back with his other paw.

Milus held up his empty paw to shield the sun from his eyes and get a clear look at the tree. The lion then took up the pose demonstrated by Heracles, held it for two seconds, spun around quickly three times, and released the stone long and fast toward the tree.

Heracles gave the lion a big pat on the back and ruffled his mane. "Yes, Lion, that was INDEED impressive," he conceded. "A heroic effort!"

Unhappy at having his mane ruffled, Milus went to lunge at the burly Greek, but Rufus and Lucia held him back.

"Careful, Milus!" warned Cornelius. "The Heracles of legend defeated many lions!"

But Milus was having none of it. "If he's so tough and legendary," he sneered, "why does he need to recruit us idiots?"

Heracles towered above Milus, his imposing size casting a great shadow over the raggedy lion. "And who says I'm going to recruit you?" he snapped. "NONE of you have yet completed my tasks!"

He leaned into Milus's face. "You came close, Lion, but you DIDN'T HIT IT!"

Suddenly Cornelius splashed into the water and found himself a big flat stone. "Let's put a stop to this nonsense, once and for all!" he squeaked.

Heracles burst into deep, rumbling laughter. "And I suppose YOU will hit it, little piglet?"

Ignoring the taunt, Cornelius took a position on the lakeside facing the tree. But he eschewed the familiar pose as displayed by Heracles and Roman jugs and adopted his own unique stance.

He held the stone tight under his belly, then skimmed it across the lake. It skipped majestically across the surface of the water all the way to the faraway tree, clattering into it with a faint *clonk*.

Heracles lifted Cornelius up high, and everyone cheered again.

"You'll need brains as well as brawn where you'll be going!" Heracles laughed.

But while everyone was caught up in the celebration, Julius spotted his brother splashing at the water's edge.

"Brutus, what are you doing?" asked Julius.

"I haven't had MY turn!" shouted Brutus as he swished his arms around. "I want to be immortal, too!"

He held up a massive rock.

"This'll do!" he declared. "WATCH ME, EVERYBODY! WATCH ME!"

Brutus stood at the edge of the lake and held up his extremely heavy rock.

Cornelius tried to stop him. "Brutus!" he shouted. "That's a completely wrong-shaped rock!"

But it was no use. Sticking out his tongue in concentration, Brutus began twirling very quickly, his rock held outstretched in his hooves.

With a deep, grunting "OOOFF!" Brutus FLUNG his boulder high into the air and over the lake, but its great size and weight meant that it didn't stay airborne for long. With a loud PLOP, the rock plunged into the water.

And with a huge ROAR, a giant hippo leaped from the lake, clutching her head in pain.

"Oh, good work, Brutus!" Julius sighed.

"RUN!" cried Brutus as everybody made a mad dash away from the angry hippo.

"NOW I'm impressed!" Heracles laughed. "You're all pretty good at running away, and there'll be PLENTY of that on my adventure!"

CHAPTER THREE
BEAST QUEST

The port of Leptis Magna, where Heracles's ship was anchored, was a few hours away. Thankfully Heracles had his own horses and cart for them all to ride on.

As Heracles drove the crew toward the port, there were grumblings of disquiet among the animals.

Cornelius shuffled up next to Julius to talk to him without being overheard. "Julius!" he whispered. "I'm really not sure why on earth we're doing this."

"To gain immortality," replied Julius just as quietly. "You heard the man."

"Yes, I know, but why us?"

"Because we're CHAMPIONS!"

"Shh!" said a panicked Cornelius, waving his hoof. "Not so loud!"

"Cornelius wants to know why we're going on an exciting adventure!" whispered Julius.

"I thought we were all going to be immortals," replied Felix.

"That's what I told him!" said Julius.

"Don't you want to be immortal, Cornelius?" asked Felix, all concerned. "It'll be amazing! Imagine living forever; I'd be able to collect every rock ever invented!"

"Imagine all the birthdays!" said Lucia, clapping.

"And all that cake!" added Felix.

Everyone nodded in approval.

"And when people ask you how old you are," said Julius, getting excited, "you could say something like, 'I am one million two thousand three hundred and thirty-two'!"

Cornelius waved everybody into a huddle, keeping one eye on Heracles, who was busy driving the cart. "It's not that part I'm unsure about," he whispered.

Something's not right.

"What concerns me is why he is asking US to do this task, as opposed to doing it himself."

"What do you mean?" asked a confused Julius.

"Well," said Cornelius, "he keeps going on about us helping him complete his 'unfinished labor'!"

"Yeah, so?" Julius shrugged. "He just needs a little assistance. No biggie!"

"But that's my point!" said Cornelius sternly. "It IS a biggie." He glanced around again at Heracles, who was happily whistling to himself unawares.

"I know all about his 'legendary' labors. They were tasked to Heracles as a PUNISHMENT, and only Heracles himself should complete them."

"If Zeus finds out he's got us idiots to help him," whispered Cornelius, "he might not look too favorably on Heracles or us, and who knows what sort of punishments he might dish out?"

"Oh, stop worrying!" pleaded Julius. "Heracles is an actual LEGEND, so he's not going to be all devious, is he?"

"You think?" replied Cornelius, not at all convinced. "Do we even know what this so-called quest is? Half of his original labors involved wrestling MONSTERS!"

"I agree with Cornelius," growled Milus. "I wouldn't trust that man as far as I could throw him."

"Well, he obviously trusts you!" Brutus sniggered. "He threw you for MILES!"

Heracles turned around to see what the fuss was. "What ails thee?" he cried, surveying the nervous-looking animals. "Have you seen ghosts?"

Cornelius was about to reply, but Julius quickly butted in. "Er, we were just wondering," he said. "Do we have to wrestle any monsters on this quest?"

Heracles burst out laughing. "No, there'll be no monsters." He snickered. "You're going to help me find an APPLE!"

"An APPLE?" blurted Julius. "Is that it?"

Julius turned to everyone in the cart. "See?" he said, smiling. "Easy-peasy!"

"Yes, but not just ANY apple!" Heracles laughed.

"A GOLDEN APPLE?" everyone cried in shock.

"Where will we find one of THOSE?" exclaimed Felix.

"This is why I require your help!" replied Heracles.

"My original apple was deemed too sacred by my meddling sister, Athena, and she returned it to the far-off land whence it came." Heracles looked off into the distance as he remembered his past labor. "It was a difficult task to acquire such a prized artifact, so I was reluctant to retrace my steps. But not two weeks ago, I was chatting to a well-traveled adventurer who had heard tell of a golden apple slipping from a warrior's pocket as he picked his way through a labyrinth."

Did you say labyrinth?!

"Yes, I did!" replied Heracles. "A HUGE maze, far too big for one man to search, so that's where you chaps come in!"

Heracles suddenly pulled on the reins and halted the horses. He looked gravely at the animals. "But you must promise me one thing," he said, and he waved them all to lean closer. "You must not tell a soul of our quest!" he whispered.

"Why not?" Cornelius asked suspiciously.

"I don't want my interfering sister finding out about it and betraying me to Zeus—I mean spoiling my surprise," replied Heracles. "Zeus loves surprises, so I want to gift him the apple myself!"

"Ooh, I love surprises!" Lucia clapped.

"Yes, and so does Zeus," said Heracles. "So keep it under your hats. NO ONE must know what we're up to!" He snapped the reins, and the horses began pulling the cart once again.

"Yeah," harrumphed Cornelius. "Apart from the fact that labyrinths are KNOWN to have monsters in them AND we have to keep quiet, there's nothing to worry about AT ALL!"

"Heracles PLAINLY said there'll be no monsters, so please stop worrying!" said Julius. "This is our best chance at being actual IMMORTAL HEROES, just like Heracles! We'll be more famous than EVER! People will sing songs about us!"

"Will we have our pictures on the side of jugs?" asked Felix excitedly.

"Almost certainly!" replied Julius.

"Oh, wow!" replied Felix. "I've always wanted to have my face on a jug!"

CHAPTER FOUR
LOYALTY PLEDGE

Before they set off, Heracles gathered everyone together.

"My friends, we are about to embark on an exciting adventure. As with all adventures, I must warn you: we may encounter great peril along the way."

"Having searched high and low throughout many lands," continued Heracles, "I have found YOU, heroes of the Roman Empire, more than worthy of the task assigned by Zeus himself and any dangers we may encounter!" He raised a fist to his chest and thumped it. "I, Heracles, son of Zeus, ask you, my newfound adventurers, to pledge your loyalty to me and the task bestowed upon us."

"We do!" Julius cried enthusiastically.

"We do?" asked Cornelius. "No one said anything about pledges!" he complained.

"If you are with me," said Heracles, "then raise your fist to your chest and swear!"

"I don't have a fist," said Brutus. "Can we use hooves?"

"Yes, of course."

"And claws?" asked Lucia.

"Yes, yes," said Heracles impatiently, "hooves, claws, paws, whatever you have."

"And if you don't want to swear?" growled Milus.

"Then you are free to leave. Although you may find it a long walk home."

"Come on, Milus!" urged Julius. "Going on an adventure wouldn't be the same without your cheery face!"

"Oh, yeah," muttered Felix, "you can't beat having a lion sitting next to you, day in, day out, to keep you on your hooves!"

Milus looked at Felix for a moment, then turned to Julius. "All right, I'll come," he said. "At the very least, I'll know I'll never go hungry." He grinned at Felix.

Heracles was getting impatient. "So, are we in agreement?" Everyone nodded. "Then put your fist—sorry, hoof, claw, paw—to your chest, and swear your loyalty!"

Cornelius raised his hoof and gave a little cough.

"Yes, Warthog," said Heracles, "you have a question?"

"Thank you," squealed Cornelius. "Now that we've pledged ourselves to you and to Zeus's task, what happens if we DON'T complete it? Does that mean we'll be in trouble with Zeus?"

"Well," said Heracles, looking very serious for a moment, "if we DON'T find the golden apple, then Zeus will banish us to Hades!" He clapped his hands enthusiastically. "So let's make sure that doesn't happen, OK?" And he bounded gleefully to the ropes mooring the ship to the jetty and untied them.

Julius shrugged. "I'm sure it's nothing to worry about!"

"NOTHING TO WORRY ABOUT!" squealed Cornelius. "You do know what HADES is, right?"

Julius looked blank for a moment. "That strange place north of Hadrian's Wall?"

Cornelius nearly exploded. "NO, JULIUS! IT'S LITERALLY IN THE PITS OF HELL! WHERE YOU GO WHEN YOU'RE DEAD!"

"Am I surrounded by NINCOMPOOPS?" screamed Cornelius.

"Do you really want me to answer that?" replied Milus dryly.

Julius tried to calm his little friend down. "Relax, Cornelius—you're making a scene!"

"Of COURSE I'm making a scene!" rasped

Cornelius. "If we don't find this stupid apple, we get sent to HELL!"

"If it's that bad," said Brutus, trying his best to help, "why don't we tell Heracles we don't want to do the quest after all?"

"Because you just swore loyalty to my cause," interjected Heracles, who had been calmly watching them squabble.

Cornelius swung around to face the Greek demigod. "You jerk!" he protested. "Why didn't you tell us about Hades before we swore loyalty?"

Because then you would've declined my invitation.

"Do not panic, little warthog," said Heracles, smiling. "Few people get banished to Hades, and some of them have even been rescued!"

"Only some?" replied Cornelius.

"Now, come on!" Heracles implored them. "Let's sail this ship out to sea!" He hauled up the anchor and directed Rufus and Lucia to hoist the sail. With Milus and Felix at the tiller, the ship finally sailed slowly out from the harbor into the open sea.

Heracles stood dramatically at the bow, one hand on his hip, the other shielding his eyes from the sun.

"Head northeast!" he declared.

We sail for CRETE!

He jumped back onto the deck. "We'll be there in three days, where this task will be swiftly accomplished!" He rubbed Cornelius's hairy head. "So put to bed any notions of failure!"

"Great," huffed Cornelius, brushing his wiry hair

back into place. "Crete. This trip keeps getting better and better. That's LITERALLY where they keep a monster in a labyrinth."

"Come on, Cornelius," said Julius. "You really need to start trusting the guy. If Heracles says there'll be no monsters, then there'll be NO monsters!"

"Old Heracles here is supposed to be a legend," retorted Cornelius, poking his hoof toward their new companion. "But what kind of legend needs help?"

"Look," said Julius, growing slightly weary of Cornelius's moaning. "If we DO find any monsters, I completely promise to tackle them first. You won't have to go anywhere near them."

Suddenly, out of the corner of his eye, Cornelius spotted something moving beside Julius's hoof.

"Look out, Julius!" he cried. "Don't step on that crab!"

Cornelius picked up the bewildered crab and plopped it safely over the side. "So much for my brave guardian!"

A flustered Julius shrugged as if nothing had happened. "Yeah, well," he mumbled, "crabs are different."

⚜ CHAPTER FIVE ⚜
HEAVY METAL

The small merchant ship sailed gently on the clear, calm surface of the beautiful deep-blue Mediterranean Sea. Julius and Cornelius stood on deck looking out toward the horizon as a gentle breeze cooled their faces.

Julius patted his old pal on the shoulder. "I know you're not into this quest, Cornelius, but I have a good feeling about this adventure!"

"How so?" asked Cornelius.

"Well, I feel we're more in control of our own destiny, don't you?"

"Not really." Cornelius shrugged.

"Oh, come on!" protested Julius. "On all our other adventures, we were THRUST into danger! Kidnapped by Romans, then thrown into the Colosseum; packed off to Britannia by Emperor Hadrian; then, to top it all off, shipwrecked in Egypt!"

Julius gazed out again across the calm sea. "I think this adventure is going to be the making of us. Because this time WE'RE in charge!"

Cornelius let out a less-than-convinced sigh. Then he looked up and saw squawking seagulls swirling above their ship.

Cornelius didn't finish his sentence. Instead he stood on tiptoe and strained his eyes, trying to get a better look at the gulls.

"Wait, what's that thing up there with the seagulls?"

Julius looked up, too. "What? That large round thing? How odd. Is it me, or is it actually getting bigger?"

Cornelius grabbed Julius by the arm and dragged him away from the ship's bow.

"IT IS! AND IT'S COMING TOWARD US!" he screamed. "RUN, JULIUS!"

"WHAT WAS THAT?" screamed Julius as he dangled helplessly over the side of the ship. Cornelius lay flat on the deck, facedown and eyes shut.

"THE SKY'S FALLING ON OUR HEADS!" squealed the little warthog. "WE'RE DOOMED! DOOMED!"

Suddenly another huge object flew in front of the sun, casting a great shadow over the ship.

"LOOK OUT!" cried Julius as he scrambled back on board. "HERE COMES ANOTHER ONE!"

As the ship bobbed and swayed from the shock waves, Rufus craned his long neck and peered in the direction of the flying boulders.

"WHAT THE HECK?" he exclaimed, giving his disbelieving eyeballs a good rub. "Look!" He pointed toward a looming shape on the horizon.

"IT'S A MASSIVE GUY, AND HE'S CHUCKING ROCKS AT US!"

"THAT WILL HIT US FOR SURE!" cried Felix as he clung to the mast. "WE HAVE TO DO SOMETHING!"

"DID YOU SAY A MASSIVE GUY?" Heracles called to Rufus.

"YES!" replied Rufus. "And judging by the way the sun glints off him, I'd say he's made of METAL!"

"WHAT?" exclaimed Julius. "You KNOW who he is?"

"Yes," replied Heracles. "He is the guardian of

Crete, protecting the island from pirates and invaders. I had hoped to escape his notice!"

"Ooh!" gasped Lucia. "Are we pirates now? How exciting!"

"BUT HOW CAN WE STOP A BIG METAL STATUE?" yelled Julius, barely able to stand as he pulled himself back over the side.

Cornelius suddenly lifted his head up from his hooves.

The little warthog leaped to his feet and scuttled over to the bow to see for himself. "Then we must get him WET!" he declared.

"WET?" spluttered Julius. "WHAT ARE YOU BABBLING ABOUT?"

"He's a big metal man. If we get him wet, he'll rust up and stop moving."

Ergo, he'll stop throwing rocks at us!

Julius looked perplexed. "But how are we going to get him wet? It's not like we have magic powers to make it rain or anything."

Everyone turned to stare at Julius.

"What?" he asked angrily. "Why are you all looking at me?"

"Well, you know," piped up Felix. "ONE of us has the power to make it rain . . ."

DON'T BE RIDICULOUS!!!

Julius stormed off to the stern of the ship. "HOW MANY TIMES DO I HAVE TO SAY IT?" he raged. "I DON'T HAVE MAGIC POWERS!"

Lucia followed the sulking zebra. "Come on, Julius," she said. "What harm could it do?"

Julius sniffed and gazed out to sea, pretending to ignore her.

"Imagine if it did work," she continued. "You'd be a hero!" She patted him on the back. "And if it didn't? Well, at least you'd have tried."

Lucia stared at the others. "You wouldn't think Julius was an idiot if it didn't work, would you?"

Heracles came over and put his arm around Julius. "Do this, and it will be your first step toward greatness!"

Julius slowly turned around. "Are you sure?" he whispered bashfully.

"YES!" bellowed Heracles confidently. "There are not many on earth who can stop Talos, but I sense you are one of them!"

Julius looked at his friends. "And are you sure you won't think I'm an idiot?"

"Of course not!" they all cried.

"GREAT!" he exclaimed, suddenly rejuvenated, and clapped his hooves.

Rufus pointed to a large silhouette standing next to what looked like a harbor. "Just on that guy there, please!"

"Righto!" agreed Julius, and immediately went into an impressive trance.

Everyone eagerly watched the heavens to see if anything stirred.

Nothing did.

Julius dropped his arms to his sides and flopped to the deck in despair. "I knew it," he groaned. "I TOLD you I didn't have magical powers."

But as his friends went over to console him, Cornelius looked up and saw another dark shadow in the sky. "Look out!" he wailed. "Another boulder!"

Expecting the worst, everyone dived for cover.

But no boulder came.

Cornelius looked up again at the sky but only saw dark gray clouds forming over the nearby island.

Then came a crack of thunder, and the heavens opened with a torrential downpour.

In the distance, a great hollow creaking noise reverberated through the air.

"That noise—it's Talos!" cried Rufus. "I think he's seizing up!"

On the horizon, the giant metal colossus swayed awkwardly as the rain began rusting up his joints.

"That's amazing!" Julius exclaimed. "Look how he's waving his arms around in despair!"

Cornelius laughed. "He's really struggling." But then the warthog took a closer look. "Wait, he's not struggling!" he squealed. "He's throwing another boulder! LOOK OUT!"

"So much for him seizing up!" cried Julius as he grabbed on to a broken piece of the ship.

Rufus bobbed next to him, holding on to the wooden fragment for dear life. "Actually," he said, peering toward the colossus, "I think he's really seized up now! Nice work!"

"Oh, yeah, great," spluttered Julius. "Well done, me."

Julius pushed off from the wreckage with his back legs. "I'm not waiting to find out how angry a dolphin can get. Come on!" And off he splashed, heading toward the harbor.

But as everyone started to swim after Julius, Cornelius spotted Heracles paddling off in the opposite direction.

"JULIUS!" Cornelius cried. "HERACLES IS GOING THE WRONG WAY!"

Julius looked around and saw Heracles disappearing off into the distance.

Heracles called out something and gave them a big wave.

"SPEAK UP!" yelled Julius. "I CAN'T HEAR YOU!"

"I think he said something about looking elsewhere for the apple," said Cornelius, straining to hear Heracles. "WHERE SHOULD WE MEET YOU, THEN?" he yelled. "SHOULD WE WAIT FOR YOU IN CRETE?"

Heracles gave a big thumbs-up, then held up two fingers.

"IN TWO DAYS?" cried Julius, trying to work out what the demigod was saying.

Heracles shook his head.

"TWO WEEKS, THEN?" guessed Cornelius.

Heracles held his thumb aloft again, then turned and kept on swimming. Soon he was just a tiny dot.

"Well, that's not weird," said Julius.

"What have I been trying to tell you?" replied Cornelius.

Julius glanced nervously at Cornelius, then, without any further comment, continued swimming toward the shore.

‹ CHAPTER SIX ›
SPA-RRING PARTNER

As Julius paddled to shore, he was amazed at how jolly and friendly the Cretan port seemed. Children splashed in the water while their parents relaxed in the hot sun. On the promenade, pretty tavernas and restaurants were dotted among the fishermen's huts. Melodic sounds of stringed instruments intertwined with the smell of food wafting from open doors.

"I could get used to this!" marveled Julius.

Lucia tugged at his arm. "Hey, Julius, check out these guys over here! How fun!"

"Hold on a second!" exclaimed Julius. "Is that our old friend PLINY?"

The little mouse leading the water aerobics fell backward into the water in shock. "WHAT?" he screamed. "Who gave your ugly mug permission to be on this island?" He leaped out of the sea and gave Julius a big hug around the neck.

"I thought you were heading back to Rome to try out your new fighting skills," said Cornelius as he embraced his old friend.

"That was the plan!" squeaked Pliny, and he dropped into the surf and ran up to Felix, who was scouring the beach for rocks.

"Oh, hello, Pliny!" said Felix.

"Watch it, bonehead!" said Pliny, jumping onto the unsuspecting antelope's head and grabbing his horns.

Brushing the sand off his paws, Pliny sauntered back up the beach to a round of applause from his old friends. "I fell in love with Crete's balmy climate and delicious grub, so I ended up staying here, learning a few more nifty moves while I was at it!" He cracked his tiny knuckles. "That's what's known as a Cretan Curler!"

Pliny pointed to a little building farther along the beach. "And now I've even got my very own health spa for retired gladiators!"

"YOUR OWN HEALTH SPA?" exclaimed Julius. "Amazing! What's a health spa?"

Pliny jumped back toward the people in the ocean and started doing jumping jacks, which they duly copied. "It's a place that helps ya keep fit and healthy in your old age! And one! And two!"

Curiosity got the better of Cornelius. "But don't you need money to open a new business?" he asked.

"Ha, ha, ha! NOTHING gets past wise old Cornelius!" Pliny said.

I'm glad SOMEONE recognizes my intelligence!

Pliny waved his arms. "After our shenanigans in Egypt, I still had a couple of them gold armbands. So, after a bit of moseying around the Mediterranean, I cashed them in, set up here, and Bob's yer uncle!"

Pliny skipped around, full of excitement to be reunited with his old pals. "Who'd have guessed I'd be so happy to see your ugly mugs?"

"So I take it old Emperor Hadrian has forgiven you, then?" Pliny asked.

"Forgiven me for what?" asked Julius, slightly confused.

"For turning down his job offer. You really upset him back in Egypt."

"They ARE?" yelped Julius, quickly ducking under the water. After a couple of seconds, he came up for air. "I can't stay under there all day!" he spluttered. "YOU HAVE TO HIDE US, PLINY!"

Pliny gave a big tut. "You GUYS!" he squeaked, scanning the beach for Romans. "What are you EVEN doing here in the FIRST place?"

"We're on a SECRET MISSION!" declared Lucia. "And I think we're going to need your help with disguises!" She rubbed her claws with glee at the prospect of exciting subterfuge.

"Ooh!" cried Pliny, backflipping off Milus's head into the soft sand. "A secret mission, you say?" He started darting around, karate-chopping the air, somersaulting backward, and kicking little rocks into the ocean as if they were dangerous foes. "I could do with a bit of a break from all this relaxing. Where are you headed?"

"The labyrinth!" Julius announced proudly.

"We're just going to pick up a golden apple!" Brutus laughed, flicking back his seaweed wig. "Easy-peasy!"

"Golden apple?" exclaimed Pliny. "There's no golden apple in the labyrinth, only a nasty Minotaur!"

"Minotaur?" echoed Julius.

"Yeah, Minotaur!" replied Pliny. "Half man, half bull. Really big monster—you don't stand a chance!"

Pliny started back to his aerobics class. "So, you can count me out."

Julius ran after him. "But please, Pliny," he pleaded. "If we don't find this apple, we're in BIG trouble. We need all the help we can get!"

Pliny looked Julius straight in the eye. "No one in their right mind goes to that dump. NO ONE!"

"But Julius has magic powers!" cried Lucia. "He stopped that big metal giant with a rain cloud this morning!"

Pliny burst out laughing. "Julius didn't stop old Talos with his magic powers," he scoffed. "Crete ALWAYS has sudden rain bursts!" He pointed to the giant silhouette in the distance. "That metal monster rusts up ALL THE TIME!"

"Then help us!" implored Julius. "You must know this place so well."

Pliny paused for a moment to ponder what madness he would be getting himself into. "Gah!" he cried. "OK, I'm in, but we HAVE to figure out some disguises, or the Romans will get you before any monster can."

The little mouse dashed toward his spa.

"This way!" he ordered, and held open a door.

As they all rushed to follow him, Julius realized someone was missing. "Where's Felix?" he asked.

"Where do you think?" Milus growled as he went inside.

Julius looked back to the beach and saw the antelope hunched over, rifling through the pebbles and rocks.

"HURRY, FELIX!" he shouted.

"Just get inside!" Julius barked, before casting a final nervous glance around the beach to make sure no Roman soldiers were watching them.

Inside, they found themselves in a hot and steamy corridor. The sound of swishing water and slapping, mixed with laughter and the odd grunt and groan, reverberated through the spa. An elderly gentleman wrapped in a wet towel squeezed past them and gave them all a polite nod.

"This place is weird!" muttered Julius.

Pliny ushered them into a small room.

"Just wait in here," he ordered, and ran off down the corridor.

"That is amazing!" gasped Brutus, peering through his seaweed locks. "What a strange and wondrous land Crete is!"

"It's a hermit crab," said Cornelius with a deflated huff.

"Ooh!" said Brutus, eyeing the crab. "A helmet crab!"

"So it's not a rock with little legs, then?" Felix sighed, poking his new find.

"No," replied Cornelius, "it's a little crab that lives in a shell."

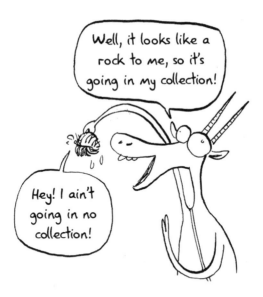

Pliny reentered the room, carrying a tower of clothes and weapons.

"We need to make tracks!" he cried, dropping the bundle on the floor. "Your arrival has already caused a bit of a stir, so we'd better scram before the local legion gets wind!"

"Where did you find this stuff?" asked Julius, admiring his long spear.

"Let's just say there's a group in the steam bath that's going to be VERY upset when they go to get dressed in five minutes," replied Pliny.

As they sneaked out the side door and onto the main road, Pliny turned to Julius and handed him a strange object.

꧁CHAPTER SEVEN꧂
AMAZEBALLS

Julius hated exercise and, as he quickly discovered, he particularly hated trudging up steep hills made of dry crumbly gravel that gave way under his hooves. The garments he was wearing didn't help, either.

Whose idea was it to go trekking up hills in heavy armor?

"You won't be moaning about wearing armor when you face that horrible Minotaur!" squeaked Pliny, who was skipping ahead. "Come on, not far now! Just over this ridge!"

"Some palace!" gasped Julius, leaning on his spear in exhaustion. "It's in ruins!"

"Yeah," replied Pliny, skipping toward the rubble, "a big earthquake took care of that!"

Come on! The labyrinth is hidden underneath!

Straightening up, Julius tramped toward the remains of the palace, followed wearily by the others.

"I can't say I like the look of this place!" said Cornelius, trying his best to keep up.

"Look," said Julius, "if this place is so old and decrepit, there's no WAY there's still a Minotaur down there!"

"I hope you're right." The little warthog sighed.

"Come on!" said Julius. "Let's grab that golden

apple, head back to one of those nice tavernas, and have ourselves a little vacay while we wait for Heracles to come back."

"You're forgetting the entire Roman army is looking for us," huffed Cornelius. "Hanging out in tavernas isn't exactly an option!"

Everyone caught up with Pliny, who was standing impatiently at the foot of the palace ruins.

The old granite door was slightly ajar, so Julius tiptoed up to the crack to see if he could peer inside. He immediately recoiled, retching. "PEEYOOO!" he cried, trying to catch his breath. "This place STINKS!"

Felix suddenly became really excited as he spotted a glinting object on the ground by the door.

"Woo-hoo!" he exclaimed. "I call the big sword!"

But as he picked it up, everyone screamed and started running away.

"SKELETON!" yelled Julius, hiding behind a big boulder.

Confused, Felix went to grab the handle of the sword, only to put his hoof on the bony remains.

Screaming, Felix ran to the big boulder behind which everyone was now hiding. "Thanks for leaving me with the skeleton hand, ya jerks!" he huffed.

With a growl, Milus stood up, pulled his helmet firmly down, raised his shield, and marched toward the entrance. "This is ridiculous!" he muttered. He put his shoulder against the heavy granite door and pushed with all his might.

Julius and the others joined Milus, and they all heaved against the dusty slab. Slowly they gathered momentum until finally, after one big SHOVE, the giant door scraped inward to reveal a long, gloomy, STINKY passageway.

"That is GROSS!" said Rufus, holding his nose. "It makes your seaweed wig seem like a bunch of fragrant flowers, Brutus!"

As the rest of them stumbled backward to catch a breath of fresh air, Julius leaned farther in, squinting at the passageway floor. "Can anyone see a golden apple? Please tell me it's right here by the door!"

Everyone inched in gingerly, gazes scouring the floor.

"It's no good," said Lucia after a moment. "I can't see a thing!" She turned around. "We need your lamp, Felix!"

But Felix was nowhere to be seen.

"FELIX?" Lucia called out. "Where ARE you?"

A timid voice piped up from behind the big boulder. "I'm not budging!"

"Oh, come on!" shouted Julius. "Stop being a baby!"

"I don't go anywhere near SKELETONS," Felix rasped. "So I'll see you when you get back!"

Cornelius trotted back to the boulder. "You know, Felix, old bones are sometimes called fossils, and fossils are in fact ROCKS!"

"Absolutely!" replied Cornelius. "Imagine how amazing your collection will look after this adventure. You'll be the envy of ALL rock collectors!"

There was a long pause before a familiar pair of horns appeared from behind the boulder and Felix bounded over to the smelly doorway. "Well, why didn't you SAY?" From his knapsack he pulled out his little oil lamp, metal striker, and pocket flint. He struck the flint and, with the spark, lit the lamp's wick.

As they nervously ventured inside, Pliny suddenly stopped Julius. "WAIT!" he cried. "Don't forget your string!"

Julius pulled out the ball from his tunic.

"Brilliant!" said Julius, holding the string firmly. "What do I do with it?"

"Oh . . . er . . . I don't know that part," spluttered Pliny. "Chuck it at the Minotaur, probably!"

"Gotcha!" replied Julius. "Then let's go find us an apple. And no Minotaur had better get in our way!"

But, just as they were about to head farther inside, Cornelius held up his hoof to stop them. "Look!" he squealed, and pointed at one of the skeletons lining the corridor. "What's that he's holding in his hand?"

Cornelius grabbed it excitedly and held it up to have a good look. "I think it's a scroll!"

"Does it tell us to go home?" asked a nervous Brutus. "'Cause I'm thinking that's a good idea."

Cornelius unrolled the old piece of parchment, and his eyes lit up. "I can't believe it!" he gasped. "What amazing luck!"

Cornelius handed the map to Julius. "Here you go, Julius," he said. "You wanted to go first, remember?"

"I did?" Julius gulped.

"Yes," said Cornelius. "You promised you'd be the first to tackle any monsters we found."

Julius nervously took the map. "Oh, yeah," he said, "so I did." He looked at the map for a while, tapping his chin. "OK," he said, "we need to go through this door."

"We've DONE that, Donkey!" growled Milus, pointing at the map. "Just lead the way!"

CHAPTER EIGHT
STRING THEORY

"This is RIDICULOUS!" Julius huffed. "We've been walking for HOURS!"

Cornelius examined a bundle of bones sitting in the corner. "Yes, I'm sure we've passed here before . . ."

I definitely recognize that face!

Milus stormed up to Julius and snatched the map out of his hooves. "How can we be lost when you have an actual MAP?"

"Yeah, all right, grumpy guts!" Julius said. "Map reading was never one of my strong points."

Milus glowered at the zebra. "Do you even HAVE a strong point?"

Milus flapped the map out flat in front of his nose and examined it carefully, then looked at the walls and passageways around them.

Julius prodded the map with his hoof. "I've been trying to get us to this part at the bottom here with the strange writing and big arrow."

Milus looked closely at the writing.

"I don't know what the words mean," continued Julius. "They're probably in really old Greek, but I bet it says something really important, like 'Here be treasure!'"

Milus looked again closely at the writing and twisted the map around one hundred and eighty degrees. He then crushed the map in one paw and slapped his forehead with the other.

"You've had the map upside down the whole time!" Milus raged.

"How dare you! No, I haven't!" Julius protested indignantly, snatching the crumpled map back. He smoothed it out, then looked at it again and at their surroundings. "Wait. How can you tell?"

Milus stabbed the map with a claw. "Because these *strange* words you've been struggling with are in fact upside-down words. Those *strange* words do in fact say, 'This way up.'"

Snarling, Milus snatched back the map and stalked to the front alongside Felix. "Everybody follow me!"

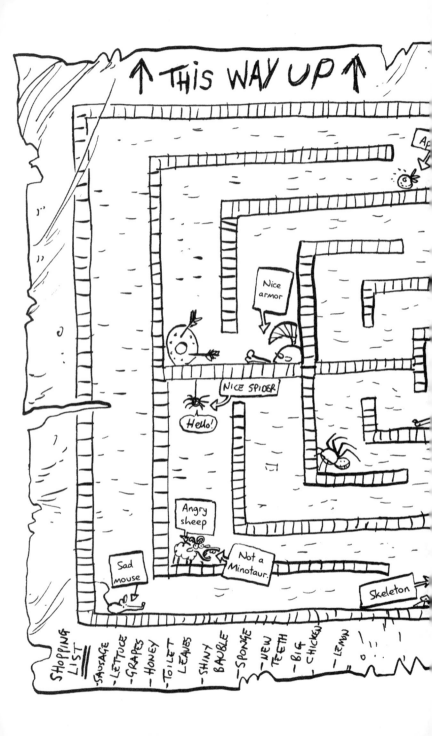

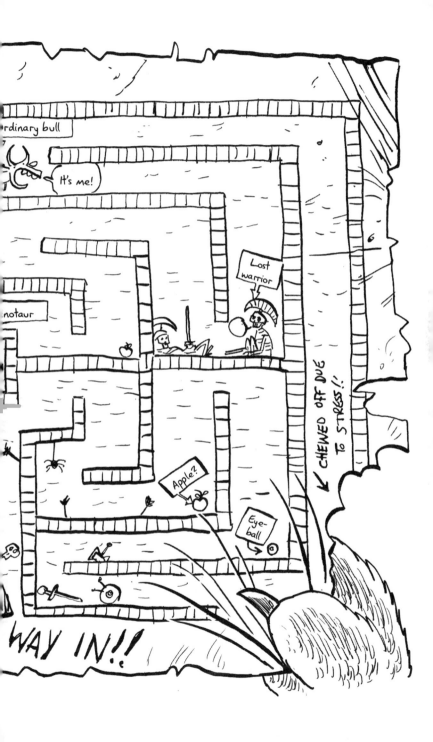

As they weaved their way through the wretched, vile-smelling passageways, Milus spotted a faint glow ahead. He held up his arm. "I think we've found him," he growled.

Julius shuffled his way to the front, holding out his ball of string. "Good work, Milus!" he declared. "I'll take over from here!"

I'll bonk him on the head with this string, grab the apple, and we'll skedaddle!

"Careful!" whispered Pliny. "They say the Minotaur is a big, nasty brute." The little mouse picked up a small rock and threw it at one of the skulls that littered the passageway. "If you're going to take him out, make sure you bonk him RIGHT on the NOGGIN!"

Julius puffed up his chest and made the meanest, toughest face he could manage. "Don't you worry about ME!" he said confidently.

I'M JULIUS ZEBRA, CHAMPION OF ROME, SAVIOR OF BRITANNIA, LIBERATOR OF ENSLAVED BEASTS, AND FORMER PHARAOH OF EGYPT!

And with that, he tiptoed off into the gloom.

"And those were his last words . . ." Felix sighed.

Before anyone had a chance to reply, they heard a shuffling noise heading quickly back down the passage. Everyone hastily pulled down their helmets and readied their shields and spears.

"It's only me!" whispered Julius. "Put your pointy spears down!"

"Did you see him?" asked Felix.

"Yes," replied Julius.

"He's at least ten times bigger than that hairy cow we fought in Britannia!" gasped Julius. "There's NO WAY I'm taking him on!"

"Then we should sneak into his lair and try to find the apple without waking him," suggested Lucia.

"Are you volunteering?" asked Milus.

"Er . . . no . . ." she replied.

"YOU should go, Donkey," growled Milus, pushing Julius forward.

"Me?" whimpered Julius. "Why me?"

Because coming here was your stupid idea in the first place!

"But he'll eat me alive!" protested Julius.

"If we're lucky," snarled Milus.

Julius looked over at the snoozing lump that was the Minotaur, then quickly surveyed the mess that surrounded the beast.

"OK," he agreed. "You're right; it was my idea to follow Heracles, and I should take responsibility."

Julius stood tall, pulled his helmet down, lifted up his shield, and crept tentatively into the waste-strewn chamber.

CHAPTER NINE
LET SLEEPING BULLS LIE

Julius crept slowly around the Minotaur's lair, on the lookout for anything apple-shaped. The floor itself was an absolute MESS! *Even worse than the dungeon under the Colosseum,* Julius thought.

Scattered about were bones, rotting food, mangled weapons, and destroyed armor. Worst of all, there was cow poop everywhere!

This Minotaur truly is a monster!

STINKY COW POOP

Something glinting in the flotsam caught Julius's eye. *It looks small and round,* he thought. *This might possibly be my lucky day!*

Carefully picking his way through the rubbish, Julius sneaked over to the suspicious object. In his haste, he accidentally kicked a small bone, which clattered against an old sword. Julius froze as the Minotaur snuffled in his sleep—disturbed, but not disturbed enough to wake.

As Julius was about to move on again, the Minotaur stirred and rolled over, old bones crunching unpleasantly beneath his solid, muscular body. He was now facing Julius, but fortunately he was still asleep, mumbling to himself as if dreaming.

Julius finally plucked up enough courage to move again. He lifted one hoof slowly over a pile of bones and tiptoed toward the shiny object he'd seen earlier.

Except it wasn't there anymore.

Something scurrying to his right caught his eye. Julius turned quickly. The shiny object was running away!

"Hey!" Julius whispered loudly. The Minotaur snorted in his sleep. Ignoring him, Julius tiptoed rapidly toward the scuttling object. Suddenly it leaped into the air and landed on the Minotaur's leg.

Julius stifled a scream!

From the other side of the chamber, Felix was watching what was happening. He patted his pockets. "Hey! I think that must be Herman, my hermit crab!" he cried. "The little devil's taken off!"

"Then you'd better go retrieve him," ordered Milus, "before your little friend gets Julius killed!"

Felix scampered toward the Minotaur. "Herman, you rascal, come back here!"

Hearing the commotion, Julius turned to see Felix blundering toward him. Frantically the zebra stuck out his hooves in an attempt to stop the antelope, but it was too late!

For a moment, Julius lay motionless in a pile of bones and cow poop, half-awake, half-concussed.

"D-do you think he heard us?" he burbled.

A great stinking, steaming mass of hair and muscle loomed over Julius.

Julius screamed and turned to flee for his life, but the Minotaur stamped his heavy hoof on Julius's tail, clamping him fast to the floor. "WHO ARE YOU THAT DISTURBS MY SLEEP?" bellowed the Minotaur. He thrust his snout into Julius's face; hot, rancid breath blasted out.

The Minotaur roared with indignation and hurled Julius against the stone wall, where he slumped to the dirt floor in a heap.

"Use the string!" called Cornelius, who was cowering with everyone else in the passageway.

Hearing Cornelius, the Minotaur turned toward the frightened animals and let out a great ROAR in their direction. "I WILL EAT EVERY LAST ONE OF YOU AND PICK MY TEETH WITH YOUR BONES!"

But as the Minotaur leaned forward, ready to charge, Julius called out boldly to the monster: "GREAT BEAST! YOU WILL NOT BE DEVOURING ANY BRAVE WARRIORS TODAY!"

The Minotaur paused and looked back at the fearless zebra.

"TODAY YOU HAVE MET YOUR MATCH! TODAY, BEAST, YOU FACE ROME'S GREATEST CHAMPION." Julius grasped for his ball of string and held it above his head. "TODAY, YOU HAVE MET JULIUS ZEBRA!"

"Oh!" gasped Julius in surprise. "I thought that was going to take him out!"

The Minotaur lunged at Julius. But this time, the nimble zebra jumped deftly out of the way.

"Throw it again!" screamed Cornelius.

Julius scrabbled around in the debris, but the ball of string had vanished. "WHERE IS IT?"

Vaulting off a fallen pillar, Julius was able to dodge the slow-moving Minotaur with ease.

He grabbed the ball from the lumbering creature. *He might be big and horrible,* thought Julius, *but he sure is SLOW!*

Julius waved the ball of string at his friends. "I'VE GOT IT!" But as he held it up triumphantly, he was jerked backward off his feet into the rubble on the floor.

"It's still attached to his horns!" cried Cornelius.

"Hold on a second," said Lucia, jumping up onto the pillar. "I've got a PLAN!" And with that, she leaped into the air and snatched the ball of string out of Julius's hoof.

"WHAT ARE YOU DOING?" shouted Julius. "YOU'LL GET YOURSELF KILLED!"

Lucia landed on a marble plinth with the string held high. "Watch THIS!" she cried.

Cornelius cleverly realized EXACTLY what the wily crocodile was up to. "COME ON, EVERYBODY!" he yelled. "LET'S HELP HER!"

The Minotaur finally collapsed in a heap on the floor, completely tangled up.

"Thank you, Lucia!" said a bruised and battered Julius. "What would we do without you?"

"I think we all need to thank YOU!" replied Lucia, dusting off her claws. "That was pretty brave, dashing in here after this brute."

Julius sauntered up to the entangled monster and held his hoof out. "Now just hand over the golden apple, Beast," he said calmly, "and we'll be off!"

The Minotaur looked confused. "Golden apple?" he growled. "What are you talking about?"

Julius blinked at him. "The golden apple! Heracles, son of Zeus, said it was down here!"

"HERACLES?" the Minotaur snorted. "What would he know? That blundering buffoon has never set foot down here!"

Cornelius cautiously approached the Minotaur, very confused. "But didn't he come down here and beat you up?" he asked. "I thought it was one of his legendary labors."

"I did get beaten up," said the Minotaur sheepishly. "But it wasn't by Heracles—he NEVER does his own labors, the lazy oaf."

Julius nearly choked. "NEVER?" he spluttered.

"Nah," said the Minotaur gruffly. "He finds some poor sap to do it for him."

HA, HA, HA! He sent YOU on one of his missions, didn't he?

Too bad!

"Like I said, he ALWAYS finds some dingbats to do his dirty work." The Minotaur laughed. "Ah, well, so long as you didn't swear the oath, you'll be all right."

He looked at the group of embarrassed faces in front of him and burst out laughing again. "Ha, ha, ha! You swore the oath! Ha, ha, ha! Too bad!"

Anyway, Heracles has sent you on a wild goose chase!

If there were a golden apple down here, do you think I'd stay in this dump?

"You really should clean this place up," said a disgruntled Julius. "It's a mess!"

"Yeah, all right!" growled the Minotaur. "Who are you, my mom?"

Julius started to trudge back toward the main passageway. "Come on, you guys. Let's go."

"But what about the golden apple?" cried Brutus.

"There isn't one." Julius sighed. "And if there is, it was never down here."

The roar of the Minotaur shook the walls of the labyrinth. "I'LL GET YOU, ZEBRA!"

Pliny dashed ahead. "That string isn't going to hold him for long. We should skedaddle!"

"Good point," said Julius. "Milus, do you have the map?"

"YOU CAN'T ESCAPE!" roared the Minotaur. "IF YOU HAD USED YOUR BALL OF STRING PROPERLY, YOU MIGHT HAVE STOOD A CHANCE!"

Everyone picked up the pace, tripping over skeletons and banging into walls in their haste.

"Used the string properly?" said Julius. "What does he mean?"

After a panicky twenty minutes, they finally spotted a welcome glint of sunlight ahead.

"We made it!" cried Felix, dashing to the door. "Quick, let's get out of here!"

The great granite door let out a huge creak as everyone squeezed through the gap and threw themselves outside into the fresh air.

"PEEYEW!" gasped Julius. "I don't know if I could have put up with that stink for one more second."

That's why you need a seaweed wig: it masks all the smells!

"Yeah," said Pliny, "but what do we get to mask the stink of YOUR HEAD?"

Julius kicked a skeleton head down the hill in frustration. "This has been an absolute DISASTER!" he moaned. "Not only is there no golden apple, but we've been hoodwinked by that jerk Heracles, and now we're all going to be banished to Heebie-Jeebies!"

"Hades," Cornelius said with an eye roll.

"That's what I said!"

Before Cornelius could reply, a strange man materialized from nowhere and stood in front of them.

"One of your friends, Pliny?" asked Julius.

"Nope," said Pliny. "Never seen him before."

"Gentlemen, I am Theseus, and I have traveled many, many miles." The strange man bowed politely. "I have unfinished business with a certain Minotaur."

Just as he spoke, a distant roar could be heard from behind the door.

"Just through there, bud," said Pliny.

Milus handed him the map. "Take this."

Theseus bowed again. "I am forever in your debt."

Before he disappeared into the labyrinth, Theseus turned to Julius and Cornelius. "I could not help but overhear that you seek a golden apple."

"Something like that." Julius sighed. "It's a lost cause now, though."

Then you must go to the Garden of the Hesperides.

There you will find many golden apples.

With that, the golden-armored Greek squeezed through the doorway.

"Wait up!" called Julius, running after him. "Where was that again?"

Theseus poked his head back around the door. "The Garden of the Hesperides."

"Hairy spiders," replied Julius.

"No," repeated Theseus. "Hesperides."

"Hairy spiders?"

"Hesperides."

"Hairy spiders."

"HESPERIDES!"

"HAIRY SPIDERS!"

"Repeat after me: Hes . . ."

"Hairy."

". . . perides"

"Spiders."

And where do we find this garden?

It is pronounced "garden," right?

"Sail west, following the glow of the sun. There you will find the Garden of the Hairy—Hesperides." Theseus then looked even more serious. "Oh, as well as the Hesperides nymphs themselves, look out for the hundred-headed dragon!"

"HUNDRED-HEADED DRAGON?" cried Cornelius.

Forget all that! It looks like we're saved!

We won't have to go to Heebie-Jeebies after all!!

"Yeah, we won't go to hell, but we do get to be eaten by a hundred-headed dragon instead. Wonderful!" Cornelius shook his head.

"We need a boat!" Milus pointed out. "Talos smashed our last one, remember?"

Pliny started skipping back down the hill. "Don't you worry about that," said the little mouse. "I've got JUST the thing!"

"Oh, stop yer moaning," said Pliny. "It gets you to where you wanna be, right?"

"So much for going incognito," growled Milus.

"Whaddya mean?" snapped Pliny. "This boat is the LAST place any Roman will look for you."

"I'll give him that," Julius said. "Even a Roman legionary wouldn't be seen dead near this boat."

"I'm STARVING!" cried Brutus, hanging over the ship's side. "I'm so hungry, I could eat my wig!"

"You can blame Milus for that," huffed Cornelius.

"Well, if we don't see land soon, even I will want to eat Brutus's wig," grumbled Julius.

Suddenly, on cue, a cry was heard from the crow's nest.

"LAND HO!" bellowed Rufus. "That fancy Greek was right—just follow the glow of the sun!"

"And we'll probably find lots of food, too, seeing as it's a garden!" said Julius cheerily.

"I think the only food served in that garden will be *us* to the million-headed dragon!" said Felix.

"Hundred-headed," said Milus.

Using their ever-improving sailing skills, the animals moored up at a small empty jetty they spotted as they entered the harbor.

Surrounding the harbor was a giant grassy slope dotted with little houses and beyond that a small mountain range.

Julius approached one of the many goats standing around eating grass.

"Excuse me, do you know where the garden of the hairy spiders is, please?" he asked politely.

"HESPERIDES!" corrected Cornelius.

"Sorry!" Julius tried again. "Hairyspuddies! Do you know it?"

The goat looked blankly at Julius while she chewed her cud. "No," she finally replied in a strange accent. "I know not of this place you desire."

But I perhaps know of a goat who does!

She turned to the other goats dotted around the hills behind her. "ARISTOPHANES!" She paused for a second, before shouting again. "ARISTOPHANES!"

One of the goats a few hundred yards away lifted his head. "Yes?"

"DO YOU KNOW OF THE PLACE THAT IS CALLED . . ." The goat turned back to Julius and stared at him.

"Oh, er . . . Hairyspuddies," said Julius nervously. "HAIRYSPUDDIES!"

Aristophanes the goat stood motionless for a while, before skipping over to his shouty friend.

Delphine, do you mean Hesperides?

SKIP!

The first goat looked at Julius. "Do I mean Hesperides?"

Julius looked at Cornelius.

"YES!" shouted Cornelius, exasperated.

"Yes!" said Julius to the goat.

The goat turned to her friend. "Yes, Aristophanes," she said calmly. "That is exactly what I mean."

"Then, Delphine, why did you not say?"

And so they headed off into the mountains, led by the two goats.

As they trekked through the rocky terrain, Milus sidled up to Julius. "When they have finished showing us the way, Donkey, you won't deny an old friend a well-deserved dinner?" He gave Julius a wink.

"NO, MILUS!" Julius whispered loudly. "You are NOT to eat our new friends!"

Milus tutted and folded his arms in a sulk. "This is going to be TORTURE!"

After a short trek traversing hidden pathways and complicated dirt trails, they approached a small glade where a warm glow emanated from beyond the trees on the other side.

The two goats gestured toward the small clearing.

"This is where we must leave you," said Delphine. "Through the trees yonder, you shall find the garden that you seek."

Aristophanes stepped forward. "If it is the golden apples that you desire, look for the glow that radiates in the darkness."

"Aren't you coming with us?" asked Julius.

"No," replied Delphine. "There are too many dangers here for a goat, and perhaps for a striped horse, too."

They all slipped behind some bushes and peeked through the branches.

"Now everyone be quiet and get down!" ordered Julius sternly. "We can't mess this up!"

Suddenly Julius spotted some movement among the trees. "There!" he whispered. "I think I saw something!"

Everyone squinted.

"I can't see anything!" Milus grunted. "This is a complete waste of time."

"Yeah!" agreed Brutus sulkily. "There's nothing but trees. You're just making it up!"

Again Julius spotted something shuffling among the trees. "Look! Didn't you see it?" he cried. "Those tree trunks seem to be moving all by themselves!"

"Wait a minute!" gasped Cornelius. "Those aren't tree trunks—they're massive LEGS!"

Julius slumped down behind his rock and let out a big sigh. "We've had it. There's no way we'll get an apple. We may as well just give up!" He kicked a small stone. "This has been a complete WASTE of time!"

"Hush!" said Lucia, who was still watching the dragon and the glade. "Someone's approaching!"

They watched the man leave. A little while later, a woman came out from the trees and walked past the dragon and up to the bundle the man had left behind.

"Ooh, look!" whispered Lucia. "She must be one of the Hesperides nymphs. They must look after the garden."

"Great," sighed Julius. "Not only do we have to

avoid a huge dragon, but we also have to sneak past some gardeners. This is the worst day of my life!"

The woman picked up the bundle, then approached the dragon and stroked one of its heads.

"Look, she's best friends with that dragon!"

"And it's not biting her head off!"

Suddenly Pliny got very excited. He leaped up onto her rock. "Hey! That gives me a GREAT idea!" he squeaked.

"Yeah, all right!" Julius said. "Chill out; you'll give us away!"

"What is it?" asked Lucia, who always loved a good plan. "Are we dressing up as nymphs?"

"In my spa, I've often heard the locals gabbing about that Trojan horse malarkey!" continued Pliny more quietly. "Do you know it?"

Julius shook his head. "Nope. Sorry, we don't do horses!"

"Yeah!" agreed Brutus, smoothing his wig with his hoof. "Horses are NINCOMPOOPS!"

"It's not a REAL horse!" replied Pliny. "It's a pretend wooden one that you give to your enemy as a present."

"Hey! We're not here to knock anyone out!" Julius protested in alarm. "We're just here to get an apple!"

"Actually, I think Pliny is on to something!" interrupted Lucia. "We should build the nymphs something like a horse, say a zebra . . ."

Lucia ignored him and continued. "We build a big wooden zebra on wheels, then give ourselves away as a present."

"We could write a nice note!" said Felix.

"Sure," said Lucia. "I guess we could."

"ANYWAY!" interjected Lucia. "As Pliny suggested, we should hide inside the zebra, steal an apple when they're not looking, then roll away to make our escape!"

CHAPTER ELEVEN

TROJAN ZEBRA

From the belly of the zebra, little Pliny's head popped out. "Are you coming up or what?" he squeaked. "It's really cozy in here!" He let down a rope, and Julius climbed up.

Lucia pulled herself up the rope next, followed by Cornelius and Brutus. Poking her head through the trapdoor, Lucia called out to Milus and Rufus.

The two of them leaned hard against the big hind legs of the wooden zebra, and it began slowly trundling across the dirt paths and grass until finally reaching the clearing. Milus and Rufus quickly hauled themselves up into the zebra before anyone spotted them.

"Good work, guys!" said Julius. "Now we just wait until someone comes and gets us!"

They didn't have to wait long. Through the small cracks in the wooden frame, Julius could see two figures approaching the zebra.

"Shush!" he said softly. "Here they come!"

Felix tried to peek through the gaps, too, but he couldn't see a thing. "What are they doing?" he whispered, shuffling sideways to get a better glimpse. "Have they found my note?"

"Keep still!" hissed Cornelius. "You'll give us away!"

With a big huff, Felix sat back down.

"My bottom!" whispered Felix. "There's a splinter in my bottom!"

"Well, it's going to have to stay there!" said Julius. "Stop shuffling around and KEEP QUIET!"

Felix tried desperately to pull the splinter out, but to no avail. "It's too small, and my hooves are like sausages!" he whimpered.

Suddenly Herman the hermit crab crawled out from Felix's knapsack, scuttled up to his bottom, and gave it a vigorous pinch.

"Thanks, Herman!" Julius murmured as the crab scurried back into Felix's knapsack.

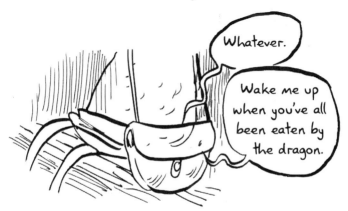

Before Julius could reply, everyone was jolted to one side. Then they all fell backward.

"I think we're moving!" whispered Julius.

Sure enough, when Julius looked through the cracks, he could see that they were rolling out of the glade and into the trees of the garden.

Julius quickly ducked and held up a hoof for silence. "Look out! We're going past the dragon!" he whispered.

I don't want to be eaten by a dragon!

Shut up, Felix!

Before long, the wooden zebra came to a standstill. At first everyone was too frightened to move, but after about five very long minutes, Julius finally worked up the courage to look through the cracks.

"Well?" Milus snarled. "There'd better be some apples, or I'm liable to start eating you all."

"Oh, stop being SO dramatic!" chided Lucia.

"Um, I can't see any apples . . ." admitted Julius. "I also can't see any nymphs."

The other animals peered through various gaps in the wooden zebra.

"Me neither!" said Pliny. "Shall we take a chance and have a look around?"

"Not it. I'm staying here!" said Felix immediately.

"But I thought you hated the splinters," said Julius.

I hate hundred-headed dragons even more!

"Yeah, I'm with Felix," said Brutus. "I'm not budging either. It's safer in here! "

"Well, if you're staying in here with me," said Felix, "you can get rid of that stinky wig!"

Brutus folded his arms and shook his head. "Wherever I go, my wig goes, too!"

"Be quiet!" whispered Julius as he shinned down the rope. Close behind him followed Cornelius, Lucia, Rufus, and Milus.

"I'll keep an eye on the wooden zebra!" Felix called out.

"Shh!" hissed Julius. "You guys are SO noisy!"

Julius did a quick scan of the garden before pointing to what looked like a small orchard. "Come on!" he said. "This looks like the place!"

They quickly sprinted to the nearest fruit trees and hid behind the trunks.

"Okeydokey," said Julius, poking his head out.
"Let's grab an apple and get out of here!"

Everyone crept out from behind their trees and
looked up into the branches and down on the ground.

"Wait," said Lucia. "What apples?"

"What do you mean?" replied Julius.

"There AREN'T any!" whispered Lucia.

"Not only are there no apples," said Cornelius, "but
there are no LEAVES, either!"

"They're not in season!" cried Cornelius. "It's early spring, and apples don't grow in spring—not even gold ones, apparently!"

Julius started banging his head against one of the trunks.

Cornelius grabbed Julius. "Stop that nonsense and come on!"

As they turned to run back to their wooden zebra, they were confronted by a group of nymphs armed with spears and shields.

"Halt, intruders!" cried one of the nymphs. "Are these the scoundrels?"

CHAPTER TWELVE

I KID YOU NOT

The nymphs marched Julius and the others into a stinky wooden pen. The hundred-headed dragon lurked in the background, slurping and licking its many lips.

"HOW COULD YOU?" cried Julius to the traitorous goat. "We thought you were HELPING us!"

Aristophanes chuckled. "For centuries we goats have been fodder for the many-headed dragon," Aristophanes sneered as he trotted around the pen's perimeter. "But I have negotiated a deal with the nymphs: if we goats bring the dragon sufficient food, then we shall be spared."

How fortunate for us that you nincompoops wandered in today!

"Good work, Donkey," grumbled Milus, slumped in the corner. "Some hero you turned out to be."

"Really, Milus?" fumed Julius, turning on the lion. "Because you've really set a fine example, what with all your constant MOANING and GROANING and SNIPING!"

"Yeah!" Brutus chipped in. "Why DO you hang out with us if you hate us all so much?"

"Milus has saved our skins more than once," Lucia pointed out, "so we should be grateful he's with us at all!"

"Yes!" agreed Cornelius diplomatically. "If Milus had wanted to stay with his friends back home, I'm sure he would have!"

Milus curled up into a tight ball like a domestic cat. "What friends?" he muttered to himself gloomily.

"Instead of fighting among ourselves," continued Lucia, "we need to think of a way out of this mess, and FAST!"

As the gang huddled together to figure out an escape plan, they suddenly became aware of a low rumbling, rattling sound.

"GOOD WORK, FELIX!" cried Julius. "EVERYONE ABOARD!"

All the animals leaped out of the pen, and one by one they swiftly climbed up the rope into the belly of the zebra.

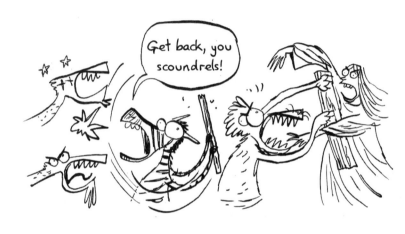

As Julius and Milus finally climbed aboard, Felix popped his head out. "Come with us, Delphine!"

"No!" she shouted back. "This is my home! And I have a few grievances to settle." With that, she confronted Aristophanes. "How dare you betray my goodwill?" she cried. "Those poor animals!"

"Now, now!" protested Aristophanes. "I was only protecting our herd—"

But as he spoke, a great beastly dragon head lunged and grabbed him in its jaws.

Suddenly Milus leaped out through the hatch and seized the back of the wooden zebra. He shouted to Delphine. "GRAB THE OTHER LEG!"

The goat ran to the other side.

"AIM FOR HIS FOOT!" ordered Milus. Together they shoved hard.

Swiftly picking up speed, the wooden zebra rolled toward the dragon, heading straight for his big gnarly toes!

Rescue mission accomplished, Milus caught up with the trundling zebra and grabbed hold of the dangling rope.

"THANK YOU, MY FRIENDS!" Delphine yelled. "I WILL NEVER FORGET YOU!"

Milus climbed back into the belly of the zebra to a round of applause from his friends.

"Good work, Milus!" cried Julius. "I'm sorry I doubted you!"

Milus shrugged. "Don't worry about it. Just worry about how we're going to stop this ridiculous contraption from rolling off that cliff!"

As the dust settled, the groaning animals hauled themselves out of the wreckage of their wooden zebra.

"Yeah, Milus!" said Pliny. "No need to get so dramatic."

Milus dusted himself down. "Dramatic or not," he huffed, "we're still no closer to finding a golden apple."

Brutus retrieved his wig from the debris and slapped it back on his head, then gave a big harrumph. "Just you wait till I see that Heracles. This whole quest has been one MASSIVE waste of time!"

Julius swatted his brother's hoof away. "I think you're forgetting that YOU couldn't stop yourself from pleading with Heracles to give you immortality, either!"

"Only because YOU were so thirsty!" retorted Brutus. "But we've been completely TRICKED!"

Brutus started to walk away from the wreckage. "That guy saw you coming a MILE off! EVERY-THING you do is a disaster! You should have 'LOSER' tattooed on your forehead to save us from getting into any more trouble!" He looked back at Julius. "With you, anything that COULD go wrong DOES go wrong."

Julius ran after Brutus and tackled him to the ground. "WHY, YOU UNGRATEFUL—!"

"Yeah!" replied Brutus. "Except everything Julius touches turns to TRASH!"

Cornelius slapped his forehead. "That's IT!" he exclaimed. "Brutus, you're a GENIUS!"

"Now, WAIT ONE MINUTE!" Julius protested. "He was being an absolute MEANIE just then!"

"I know, I know!" replied Cornelius. "But he may have just saved the day, and our friend Heracles, too!"

Julius was confused. "Cornelius, what are you BLATHERING on about?"

"Isn't it obvious?"

We pay a visit to King Midas!

⸸ CHAPTER THIRTEEN ⸸
GET KNOTTED

The journey to Midas City was a touchy, awkward affair. Brutus had made Julius feel like a failure, and being stuck on a tiny ship with someone grumpy is not ideal at the best of times.

Julius looked wistfully up at the sail as it fluttered in the wind. "I had hoped these adventures would bring us closer. Brutus has his moments of pigheadedness, but then he seems to come around and actually be a good friend and brother."

Cornelius patted his friend on the back. "You're younger than he is, and he sees you doing well in the world. Of course he's going to lash out! He's jealous."

"Maybe he's right, though," sighed Julius. "Maybe I have made a mess of things."

"Are you sure we're going the right way, Pliny?" called out Cornelius. "It's been two days since our stopover at Crete."

"Yes! Not far now!" squeaked Pliny. "A few more hours, then we should reach the port of Attalea." He skipped over to Julius and Cornelius. "We have to be EXTREMELY careful, though. Attalea is a very Roman port these days. They say Hadrian himself visited not so long ago."

He pulled on a hooded top. "We'll have to be disguised," he told them, tugging the hood low over his face. "You guys stay on the ship while I buy us a horse and cart for the five-day trip to Phrygia, where we'll find Midas's palace."

As Pliny had told them, it was another few hours before they finally reached Attalea. Everyone hid below deck while Pliny scampered off to find them transport.

"Wait there! I won't be long!" the little mouse said.

As Pliny skipped off, Julius poked his head up above deck to have a peek at the port. But with a yelp, he quickly ducked back down.

"What is it?" asked Lucia.

Julius gasped. "Pliny wasn't kidding! There are Romans EVERYWHERE!"

Rufus poked his head up to have a look, too.

"WHAT?" cried Julius.

"SHH!" warned Cornelius. "Now's definitely not the time to draw attention to ourselves!"

"Too late!" said Rufus, quickly withdrawing his neck. "Someone's coming!"

"Pliny?"

"Romans!"

Everyone sat very still, listening for any noise. Suddenly there was a sharp rap on the side of the ship.

"Hello?" called a voice. "We need to see your papers!"

"We've had it!" whispered Felix. "They'll throw us to the lions!"

Footsteps thumped on the deck above their heads. As everybody froze, Lucia suddenly leaped up. "I've got this!" she whispered.

The two soldiers drew their swords and pointed them at the crocodile.

"We need to see your papers," one said sternly. "You have to have a license to moor here."

"Oh, boys, boys!" Lucia exclaimed. "You both look so stressed!" She pointed to the big signs painted on the hull and sail. "You have definitely come to the right boat!"

Before they could answer, she grabbed one of the soldiers and made him lie facedown flat on the deck.

The second soldier looked on, bemused. "Um, can I have a turn next? I've got a super stiff neck!"

"Of course, of course!" replied Lucia. She turned to the hatch. "PERHAPS ONE OF MY ASSISTANTS COULD HELP?"

There was the sound of scuffling and whispers of "You go!" and "No, YOU go!" before the familiar face of Milus popped up above deck.

"How may I be of service?" he snarled.

Suddenly little Pliny jumped on board, carrying a bundle of blankets. He nearly fainted at the sight before him.

The soldiers hastily pushed Lucia and Milus away, jumped up, and drew their swords on Pliny.

"IS THIS YOUR BOAT? WHERE ARE YOUR PAPERS?"

Pliny rushed to placate them. "Gentlemen! Calm down!" he said. "I see you have sampled our world-famous services."

The two soldiers looked at each other, then back at Pliny. "You've got half an hour, Mouse," barked one of them, "and when we return, I want you to do my feet!" He leaned into Pliny's face. "DO I MAKE MYSELF CLEAR?"

"As a bell!" replied Pliny. "Your feet will love you forever!"

As the two soldiers left the ship, Pliny fell into a heap on the floor.

Julius jumped up on deck. "Good work, you three!" He laughed. "I thought we were goners for sure!"

Pliny picked up the blankets and threw them at his friends. "Put these over your heads and come with me. We have to get out of here before those soldiers come back." He leaped off the boat and started to head up the road. "Hurry! This way! I've got a cart and a couple of horses!"

Down an old back alley, they found two horses reined to a cart.

"Jump in the back and I'll throw that big blanket over you!" said Pliny. "We'll be safe once we're out of the city."

CHAPTER FOURTEEN

DON'T GET TOUCHY

Once the group got past the city walls, the journey was Roman-free. Apart from the odd traveler and gang of bandits, the animals' ride was smooth sailing.

As they trundled along in their cart through a particularly dense stretch of forest, Julius jumped up and clapped his hooves together.

"Now, listen up, everyone!" he called. "I know things have been tough, and you were probably all expecting this to be over by now."

"ANYWAY!" said Julius. "We only have a few hours of journey left, so I think, to celebrate, we should have a SING-ALONG!"

"Can we *not* sing zebra songs?" Pliny pleaded. "We ALWAYS sing stupid zebra songs!"

Julius put up his hooves. "You can sing whatever you like! Even mouse songs!"

They all sat there thinking for a moment, racking their brains for a good song.

Suddenly little Herman the hermit crab crawled out of Felix's knapsack. He scuttled along the side of the cart and stopped at the back on top of a bale of hay.

He perched there silently for a moment, then nervously cleared his throat. He tapped his claws to get a rhythm, then burst into song.

"One, two, three, four, five, once I caught a fish alive!"

"That's the ticket!" Julius laughed. "All hail HERMAN THE HERMIT CRAB!"

As they whiled away the hours with all sorts of merry songs, the forest began to thin out until they could finally see a gleaming white-and-gold palace on the hillside ahead.

"Ooh!" cried Julius. "That MUST be it!"

Everyone turned to look.

As they climbed the steep hill, they drove their cart up to the huge wooden doors of the perimeter wall.

Julius jumped out and examined the colossal doors. "What do we do?" he asked. He turned to the others and gave a shrug. "Just knock?"

Milus remained unconvinced by the whole plan. "I still say this is ridiculous," he growled. "What are we going to do when we see him? Say, 'Excuse me, do you mind turning an apple into gold, please? Thank you!'"

Lucia was less than convinced, too. "What if he doesn't even have the power? What if it's all some stupid legend? Heracles is hardly living up to his legendary status so far."

"Yeah!" Felix chimed in. "Midas might have us EXECUTED just for ASKING!"

A huge creak interrupted Felix's whining, and a guard looked out.

"Who dares knock on the doors of MIDAS?"

"See! I told ya!" whispered Felix, lying low in the cart. "We're all DOOMED!"

The guard looked Julius up and down, cast a glance at the frightened animals in the cart, then looked back at Julius.

"Wait here," he commanded, and he then disappeared, closing the doors firmly behind him with a great BOOM!

Julius turned back to his friends and gave another shrug.

After ten long minutes, the doors opened once again, making Julius nearly jump out of his skin.

The soldier stood proudly by the open doorway. "His Majesty, King Midas, welcomes Lord Julius and his companions and invites them to dine with him this evening."

With the cart in tow, Julius entered a grand courtyard with flagstones of many fantastic and intricate patterns. Dotted everywhere were trees and plants of all shapes and sizes and colors. Occasionally, sitting among the plants, golden objects glinted in the sun. Everyone climbed out of the cart to take a closer look, only to find perfectly carved and realistic golden animals that seemed like they would jump at you at any moment.

"Check out these sculptures!" said Julius. "This squirrel looks so real."

"Come," ordered the guard. "Do not delay any further. The king awaits."

He led them away from the courtyard down a long passageway, golden statues lined up on either side.

Cornelius was also eyeing the statues as they walked. "Is it just me, or are their poses a bit weird?" he muttered to Julius.

"How do you mean?"

"Well," continued the little warthog, "normally a statue is a celebration of somebody in a regal pose, you know—waving, or looking important."

Julius and Cornelius looked at each other in horror the truth dawned on them. They stepped away from the statue and caught up with the rest of the party, who had arrived at some grand, ornate double doors. The guard banged on one with the hilt of his sword.

The heavy thumping echoed down the passageway and around the cavernous palace.

Almost immediately the doors swung open and revealed a magnificent-looking banquet hall with an impressive long table down the middle, cutlery and crockery already laid out.

A young, bearded man greeted them. "Come in! Come in!" He was dressed in smart, colorful woven robes and wore a shiny golden crown.

"What an honor!" he declared. "What. An. HONOR!"

He made a beeline toward Julius and held out his hand to greet him. "It's very exciting to meet you, Lord Julius." Immediately Julius flinched and pulled his hoof away.

Julius hastily grasped the king's hand and shook it vigorously. "No, no!" he said. "The pleasure is all mine! All mine!"

Felix turned to Brutus. "Why are they repeating everything?" he whispered.

"It must be the fancy way of doing things," replied Brutus.

Meanwhile, in his nervousness, Julius had gripped King Midas's hand so tightly that when Midas withdrew it, the glove was left in Julius's clenched hoof.

"Come, come!" said the king, slipping his glove back on as if nothing had happened. He motioned to the huge table. "Take a seat. You are obviously exhausted from your arduous journey!"

"Yes, sorry, sorry," stammered Julius. "We, er . . . met lots of bandits on the way. My nerves are a bit on edge."

"Of course," replied the king graciously.

As everyone pulled out a chair, King Midas clicked his gloved fingers and food was immediately served.

"A king must ALWAYS be prepared!" said Midas. He snapped his fingers again and a small group of musicians gathered in one corner and began playing traditional Greek folk music.

"Oh, how lovely!" Felix slurped a mouthful of food. "We were only having a sing-along ourselves half an hour ago, weren't we, Julius?"

"Oh, really?" asked the king. "Pray tell what tunes you have brought from Rome and Egypt!"

"Do you know the one about a fish being caught alive?" replied Felix.

"Not now!" interjected Julius. "King Midas doesn't want to hear about your hermit crab's nonsense!"

"Perhaps later," said the king, still excited to receive guests in his palace. "Tell me about YOU, Lord Julius." He smiled at Julius. "Your fame has reached even these remote hills of Phrygia!"

Midas took a sip of his wine. "Is it true you have bested that Roman scoundrel Hadrian TWICE, and ruled Egypt to boot? Very impressive, I must say."

The banquet hall went very quiet as Julius choked on the lettuce leaf he was chewing. "GOSH, NO!" he spluttered. "Not at ALL!" He grabbed a napkin and nervously wiped his face.

The king stared intently at Julius before breaking into a smile, then a chuckle, then outright laughter. "HA, HA, HA, HA, HA, HA!" he roared, slapping Julius on the back. "YOU SHOULD HAVE SEEN YOUR FACE!"

Julius and his friends all began laughing along nervously, looking sideways at one another, wondering what the joke was.

"Ha, ha, ha!" Julius laughed weakly. "You got me there!"

The king suddenly stopped laughing. "But tell me honestly—why ARE you here?"

What brings the superstar Julius Zebra to my halls?

"Well, you know," said Julius, popping another lettuce leaf into his mouth and glancing anxiously at his friends. "We were on our vacay in Greece . . ."

"Vacay?" repeated a confused Midas.

"Yeah, vacay," confirmed Julius. "We saw a bit of Crete, went to a spa."

Pliny gave a wave. "My spa!"

Midas raised an eyebrow and nodded in approval.

"And we wondered," continued Julius, "what great Greek legend should we visit?"

"What indeed!" agreed Midas.

"And we all said, 'Yeah, what a great idea!' and so here we are!"

"Well, I am glad you did, and I thank you for the company." Midas raised his glass before taking another sip.

He flopped back in his chair with a sigh. "We don't get many visitors," he said, "but my burden"—he held up a gloved hand—"or should I say my CURSE?—does rather lure the curious."

The banquet hall fell silent again.

"So, er, the stories *are* true?" asked Julius. "You are truly cursed with a golden touch?"

Midas gazed at Julius, a scornful look in his eye. "Yes," he whispered. "And it's not easy."

He held up one hand. "These lead-lined gloves help, but they cannot always be trusted to stave off the curse."

"You know," said Midas, "the worst of it—and you'll understand this, Julius—is people

DEMANDING I turn things to gold, like I'm some sort of performing MONKEY!"

Julius laughed nervously. "Oh, er, jeez! Ha, ha, ha!" he stammered. "That must be AWFUL!"

"You probably saw my collections of those who dared ask me to perform such a trick!"

Julius risked a frightened sideways glance at Cornelius.

At that moment, across the table, Brutus stood up holding a big green apple in his hoof. "Saying that, though," he began, flipping the apple into the air and catching it again.

"Yes?" asked Midas, a frown furrowing his brow.

"You see this apple?"

"What of it?" growled Midas.

"BRUTUS!" shouted Julius. "Not now!"

Brutus has his own party trick of stuffing an apple in his mouth and shutting up for the rest of the evening!

Gluh!

"Interesting . . ." Midas murmured.

"ANYWAY!" Julius cut in, raising his goblet. "Let's drink to us poor celebrities and our troublesome fans!"

Midas drained his goblet, then stood up and began swaying to the jolly folk music. "Come, Julius!" he cried. "Dance with me!"

Julius choked on his food again. "What? REALLY?"

"YES! YES!" Midas crowed with a laugh. "ALL of you! Here in Phrygia it is customary to dance after dinner!"

"This I gotta see!" scoffed Milus, slouching in his chair.

"You too, Lion!" insisted Midas, roughly dragging the reluctant beast onto his feet.

CHAPTER FIFTEEN
GOLDEN BOY

"What time is it?" asked Julius.

Cornelius looked out the nearest window at the stars. "Almost certainly past midnight."

"This is probably the latest I've EVER stayed up." Julius yawned.

In the corner, the musicians were still playing their folk songs, and Felix, Pliny, and Rufus were throwing down in a desperate attempt at Greek dancing.

"Guys!" Julius called out. "Give those poor musicians a rest and come sit down!"

The animals reluctantly came back to the table and sat down, while the musicians packed up, made their farewells, and left for bed.

Brutus, sitting opposite his brother, leaned over the table and whispered, "So, are we going to do it now or what?"

"Do what?" Julius whispered back, holding up a hoof to shush him.

"Duh! Get him to touch an apple!" said Brutus. "Why else are we here?"

"You heard the man," Julius whispered. "He doesn't like being asked to use his powers. Did you see those statues outside? We'll just have to find another way."

Brutus huffed and flopped back into his chair. He glared at Julius while popping grapes into his mouth. Suddenly he leaped onto the table, grabbed an apple, and made a beeline for the snoozing Midas.

Brutus hopped off the table beside Midas. "I'm going to do it!" he declared. "We didn't travel hundreds of miles just to dance to weird music!" He bent down beside Midas's chair and started to tug at one of the king's gloves.

Julius was beside himself with distress. "BRUTUS!" he hissed loudly. "Step away now, or I won't be responsible for my actions!"

Milus bounded onto the table and thrust a spear toward Brutus.

Brutus looked coolly at Milus, then, with a swift flick, pulled the glove off and tossed it over his shoulder.

Everyone let out a gasp as Milus's spear pressed against Brutus's throat. Without breaking a sweat, Brutus slowly held up a golden, gleaming apple. "There!" he said, throwing it to Milus. "It's done. Now we can go!"

Milus inspected the apple. "That is actually quite impressive, Donkey." He threw it to Julius.

Julius also examined the apple, then looked up crossly at Brutus. "You idiot! You'll be the death of us!"

He stuffed the apple into his tunic pouch and stood up slowly from his chair. Luckily Midas was still fast asleep.

Felix and Rufus trotted over to have a look. "Show us how you did it!" begged Felix. "We want to see!"

"No!" said Julius emphatically. "We're in enough trouble. We need to GO!"

Ignoring him, Felix grabbed a banana from the fruit bowl and touched it against Midas's bare finger.

Not wanting to be left out, Rufus searched for something else to turn into gold. He quickly grabbed Brutus's stinky seaweed wig and brushed it against Midas's hand. The wig turned to solid gold.

"Hey, you jerk, that's mine," protested Brutus, but as he went to grab it back, his hoof caught Midas's thumb, and he turned instantly into a statue of gold.

As they all stood frozen in shock, the huge doors opened and the guard from earlier walked in. "The guest rooms are ready—" He stopped in his tracks, taking in the scene before him. "WHAT IN THE NAME OF—?"

"We have to go now, or we're ALL dead."

CHAPTER SIXTEEN

HE AIN'T HEAVY...

Julius, Milus, and Rufus all grabbed hold of Brutus and heaved him toward the door.

"This is ridiculous!" cried Julius. "He weighs a flippin' TON!"

Lucia ran to one of the long red velvet curtains hanging at the grand windows and ripped it from its rod, sending curtain rings flying everywhere.

She dragged the curtain over to Brutus. "Lay him on here," she said.

As they dragged Brutus through the doors and out into the corridor, Midas began to stir. "Wh-where's everyone gone . . . ?" he murmured drowsily.

Lucia and Rufus slammed the doors, and Lucia slipped her spear through the handles, sealing the doors.

"LOOK AT THE DOORS!" cried Rufus.

Everyone spun around to see what the giraffe was shouting about.

"THEY'VE TURNED GOLD!" squealed Cornelius.

A great roar erupted from the banquet hall as Midas realized what had happened.

"WAIT TILL I GET MY HANDS ON YOU!"

he bellowed. "YOU'LL BE STANDING IN MY STATUE COLLECTION WITH THE REST OF THE THIEVING SCOUNDRELS!"

"Can't we move him any quicker?" wheezed Julius. "I don't want to end up as a statue, too!"

"We've got to get him down these steps first!" said Lucia.

"Try not to break him!" Julius was panicking. "I know he's an idiot, but he's MY idiot!"

They carefully placed Brutus on the top step.

"Now, be gentle," said Julius. "One step at a time!"

Everyone knelt behind Brutus and waited for the command.

"Hurry up!" urged Cornelius. "His guards will be here any second!"

"One," continued Julius, "two . . . THREE!"

Everyone raced after the gold Brutus, trying to catch him before he did any more damage.

"GRAB HIM!" cried Julius. "HE'LL LOSE A NOSE OR AN ARM OR SOMETHING!"

As the rolling Brutus reached the doors at the end, three guards appeared. "STOP, OR FACE DEATH!" they shouted.

"Good work, Brutus!" Julius exclaimed as his brother smashed through the front doors.

"Is it me," said Milus, "or is Brutus far more useful as a statue than as a living, breathing zebra?"

Everyone rushed through the doors. Brutus had finally come to a stop in the courtyard.

"Where's our ride?" Julius cried. "We have to get out of here quick!"

"Stop worrying!" said Pliny, leaping into action. "Watch this!"

Almost immediately the horses and cart pulled up out of nowhere.

"Good work!" cried Julius in relief.

"All horses and carts come with a free whistle upgrade these days," revealed Pliny. "We're truly living in the future!"

Once Brutus was finally loaded, everyone else jumped on and Pliny flicked the reins. "Giddy-up!" he cried. "Back to port for us!"

As they zipped off, they heard a voice yelling at them from behind.

"As if we weren't in ENOUGH trouble with Rome!" Julius sighed and rested his hoof on the frozen golden figure of Brutus. "Oh, brother, what trouble you have brought upon us . . ."

"Well, he did do ONE good thing before he . . . er . . . went," said Cornelius.

Julius didn't look up from stroking his poor brother. "No, Cornelius," he said quietly. "This quest is far from over."

"What do you mean?" Cornelius exclaimed. "We have the apple!"

"Yes, but I've lost my brother," replied Julius. "And I intend to get him back!"

"Get him back? HOW?"

"If my brother is dead, then he must already be in Hades."

CHAPTER SEVENTEEN
JOURNEY TO THE UNDERWORLD

Sailing to the fabled underworld couldn't be the easiest of tasks, but Julius remembered Heracles saying that he'd heard of people being rescued from there, so he knew it was possible.

After much searching and asking around in Attalea, then back in Pliny's home of Crete, the animals had managed to track down an old map that purportedly showed the way to Hades.

This really is a long shot, Julius. Any fool could have drawn this!

"I know," replied Julius, "but it's all we have." He looked out toward the darkening storm clouds. "If Heracles says people can be rescued from Hades, then we have to try!"

A chill wind blew across the sea, and on deck everyone pulled their blankets tighter over their heads and shoulders. They had reached the mouth of the dark river Styx, which was marked on their map.

The river twisted and turned through a forbidding, misty landscape as haggard crows cawed at them from rotten trees. Everyone clutched their swords tighter, ready for any danger.

As they slowly sailed around another bend, the river widened and revealed the mouth of a pitch-black lake.

Felix gasped. "I DEFINITELY think we've found the right place."

In the distance was a dock with a small boat tied up at the end.

Cornelius glanced at the map. "Head for that dock," he said decisively.

That's where we'll find the ferryman!

They climbed out onto the creaky, ramshackle dock.

"Be careful!" Julius warned. "These planks are falling apart!"

They gingerly walked across to the small rowboat with its mysterious passenger.

Julius approached the hooded figure warily. "Excuse me, are you the ferryman?"

Cornelius consulted his map again. "He's called Charon," he whispered.

Julius cleared his throat. "Are you the one they call Sharon?"

The figure didn't speak or move. Only the gentle lapping of the water broke the silence.

Julius turned to the others and shrugged. He tried again. "Excuse me—"

An icy voice floated on the breeze from the lake.

Charon.

Julius pulled his blanket tighter around his shoulders and let out a little *brrr*. "I'm sorry," he said. "What did you say?"

There was a pause before another icy whisper drifted from the hood. "My name is *Charon*."

"I have an Auntie Sharon!" Felix piped up.

Julius turned around and put his hoof to his mouth to shush Felix.

"Listen, Sharon," said Julius carefully. "I need to cross this lake to find my brother, and I've been told that you can help me."

In reply, Charon held out a bony hand.

"He needs payment!" said Cornelius.

Julius showed him the golden apple. "Will this do?"

"No, Julius!" hissed Cornelius. "Give him a coin."

"This is all I've got," replied Julius. "And there's no point in keeping it if I can't have my brother back."

Julius carefully placed the golden apple in Charon's hand.

Charon raised the apple to his hood and held it there as if examining it. He then set it beside him.

There was a long, awkward pause.

"Is that a yes?" asked Julius eventually.

"I think that's a yes!" said Cornelius.

Once they were all settled, Charon began slowly rowing across the great expanse of lake.

As they glided across the lake, Julius was amazed at how still the surface was. The only ripples came from their boat. There was not a sound to be heard: no birds in the sky, no rustling of the wind. Only the gentle splash of the oars dipping in the water broke the silence.

Before long, a dark shadow of land loomed menacingly through the mist. As they drew closer, Julius saw that it was a mountainous, foreboding land, devoid of color and life. Dead, gnarly trees sat among ravaged boulders.

Charon stopped rowing as they glided to the shore, and everyone stepped off into the shallows and made their way to dry land.

The ferryman reached out as Julius passed and seized him by the arm.

He tugged Julius closer. "Take this lyre," he hissed, passing him a small stringed instrument. "It will soothe the darkest of souls."

Julius went to move away, but Charon held on to him tight. "Once you find your brother," he hissed, "do not look back at him as you pass back through the gate, not until you reach my boat."

"Thank you, Sharon." Julius gulped.

You are most welcome ... Julia.

CHAPTER EIGHTEEN
SPIRITED AWAY

"Right," said Julius, walking up the hill, "let's get this over and done with as quickly as possible. I don't want to stay in this place any longer than I have to."

He pointed to the gate in the distance. "He says we'll find Brutus through there, so let's go!"

Felix held up a smooth round gray stone. "You can't visit the netherworld and not collect a rock. I wouldn't be able to forgive myself!"

In the corner of Julius's eye, a shadow flitted between the rocks and trees behind Felix.

"Well, if you want to stay here with all the ghosts and ghoulies," said Julius, "then that's up to you!"

Felix spun around and saw a lurking figure, then hastily stood up and plopped his stone in his knapsack.

They dashed toward the others, who were crouched down near the ancient, crumbling stone gate.

Julius ran up the path right past them. "Come on!" urged Julius. "What are you all doing hiding behind those rocks? Let's not dillydally!"

Wait! There seems to be some sort of big dog guarding the gate!

"Big dog?" Julius blurted out as he skidded to a halt on the gravel. He ran back to where Cornelius was hiding behind a boulder. "He never mentioned anything about a guard dog!"

"This is no ordinary dog, either," said Cornelius.

"But there are seven of us," exclaimed Julius. "Surely we can tackle a single dog between us." Julius suddenly heard a loud snuffling and low growling coming from the gate. He decided to have a peek around the boulder to see exactly what it was.

"Well, that's that!" said Julius, slumping against the boulder. "We're not getting past THAT thing!"

Lucia came and sat next to her friend. "Come on, Julius. There's ALWAYS a way!"

Julius appreciated the sentiment, but he shook his head. "I know you can usually find a way out of a tight spot, Lucia, but I think we've had it this time."

Lucia wasn't having any of it. She picked up the lyre that Charon had given him. "What's this for?" she asked.

"Oh, What's-his-name said it would 'soothe the darkest of souls' or something."

"Huh!" replied Lucia, and she started plucking at the strings. A beautiful tune began to play by itself.

Sitting on a boulder next to them, Milus immediately fell asleep and began snoring.

"Hey! What happened to the sourpuss?" asked Pliny, pointing at Milus. "He fell asleep!"

Julius took the lyre and held it up to have a good look. "That. Is. AMAZING!"

Julius carefully crouched behind a large boulder farther up the path and waited for the big dog to come his way as it paced up and down in front of the gate. As soon as the snuffling and growling grew louder, Julius leaped out in front of the beast and began playing the lyre.

The big dog came to a halt, and all six of its eyelids began to droop. The soothing sound of the lyre seemed to be doing the trick!

Eager to speed things up, Julius decided to sing along to the melody.

Unfortunately Julius's nasal caterwauling only served to wake the creature from its drowsiness. With a great ROAR, it shook its three heads and turned to Julius, its eyes red with fury.

"STOP SINGING!" squealed Cornelius. "YOU'RE UPSETTING IT!"

"You're upsetting me, too!" complained Pliny, his paws stuffed in his ears.

"Well, THAT'S rude!" huffed Julius, but he stopped his warbling and let the lyre play on its own.

Once again, the monster dog started to relax, and finally it flopped to the ground in a sluggish slumber.

Julius sneaked over just to make sure.

He motioned everyone to come forward, and they all tiptoed past the snoozing beast.

Once through the gate, they discovered a world of ancient crumbling ruins among the long-dead trees. The fog was thicker and gloomier here, and the cold, damp air chilled their bones.

"How on earth are we going to find him out HERE?" wailed Julius. In desperation, he called out his brother's name.

Julius's voice echoed through the murkiness, but no reply came. Some of the others began calling out Brutus's name, too, as they wandered through the mist.

Just as all seemed lost, Rufus cried out from a clump of gnarled tree stumps just ahead.

"Over here, Julius!" he called. "I think I can see someone!"

Everyone ran toward Rufus, and sure enough, a shadowy figure seemed to be walking toward them through the gloom.

"Brutus?" Julius called out excitedly. "Is that you?"

As the animals turned to flee, they saw more skeletons marching toward them, each dressed up in decayed tunics and armor.

"KEEP IT DOWN!" they bellowed, waving their rusty swords and spears.

As fearsome as it looked, the skeleton army was fortunately no match for Julius and his well-trained friends.

"This is easy!" Rufus laughed as he bashed up two flimsy skeletons at once.

Lucia was leaping off the ruins and knocking the undead into countless pieces. "Yes, but there are SO many of them!"

But poor Julius was starting to get frantic. "This is distracting us from our mission!" he cried. "We need to lose this skeleton horde!"

"I'm with you!" said a familiar voice.

Julius gave his long-lost brother a big hug.

"Hey!" protested Brutus, trying to push him off. "What are you doing?"

"What am *I* doing?" laughed Julius. "What are YOU doing? How did you find us?"

"I'm not sure," admitted Brutus, rubbing his head. "One minute I'm turning apples into gold. The next I'm stuck here with this stinky bunch!"

As he pushed the skeleton away, Brutus grabbed Julius desperately by the shoulder. "Brother, where IS this place?"

"Best not to ask!" replied Julius. "Come on, we've got to go!"

Julius jumped onto a big boulder and held up his sword. "Everyone, great news! I've found Brutus!" he announced. "Let's leave these skeletons and head back to Sharon!"

As the others ran off, a tired Brutus found himself caught up in a tangle of skeletons. "JULIUS!" he cried breathlessly. "DON'T LEAVE WITHOUT ME!"

Julius turned back and hauled him out of the bony melee. "This way, Brutus. I'm not about to lose you twice!"

Throwing his arm around his brother, Julius led Brutus away from the skeleton mob and toward the giant stone gates. As they approached the gateway, Julius hid cautiously to the side.

"Careful here," Julius warned. "We have to watch for a big three-headed guard dog!" He peered around the crumbling column. "Hopefully he's still asleep."

But before Julius crossed the gate threshold, he remembered the warning.

Do not look back at him as you pass back through the gate, not until you reach my boat.

Julius took a deep breath before running out through the gateway and past the snoring monster dog. "This way, Brutus!" he called out, careful not to look back. "We're nearly there!"

But Brutus didn't reply.

Julius started to panic. *What if he's been recaptured by the skeletons?* he thought. *How am I supposed to help him if I'm not allowed to look back at him?* He tried calling out to his brother again, "Hey Brutus, can you imagine what Mom's going to say after we tell her about our bonkers adventures?" He laughed. "She'll go bananas, right, Brutus?"

Again, no reply.

It was no good; Julius couldn't bear it. *What if my brother really is in trouble?* he thought. *I couldn't live with myself if I left him behind in this rotten place!* Julius stopped running. *What's the worst that could happen if I look back, anyway?*

So he turned around. "Brutus, are you all right?"

And there, right as rain, was Brutus. He was running right behind him, deep in concentration, and picking his nose.

Suddenly, as Brutus wiped his booger on a nearby rock, he started to turn a strange grayish blue. "Hey! What's happening?" he cried.

Brutus reached out his hoof to Julius, but, like a wisp of smoke slowly dispersing in the wind, he was gone.

CHAPTER NINETEEN
JOURNEY'S END

Julius walked dejectedly back to the boat.

"Where's Brutus?" asked Cornelius.

"Gone," replied Julius.

"Gone?" Cornelius gasped. "Gone where?"

Julius climbed aboard the boat and slumped against the side.

"Yeah, OK," snapped Julius. "No one likes a know-it-all."

Lucia jumped up and unsheathed her sword. "Well, what are we waiting for?" She leaped into the water and waded to the shore. "Let's get him back!"

Charon let out an icy hiss. "None that are living may pass through the gates of Hades twice."

Everyone shivered as Charon's icy words chilled the air.

"I bet he's a hoot at parties," whispered Pliny to Milus.

Lucia reluctantly returned to her friends, and Charon rowed the little boat back across the lifeless lake.

"We've completely failed," Julius said with a heavy sigh. "Not only have we lost Brutus, but we don't even have the golden apple!"

They finally reached the shore and were glad to see that their ship was still there waiting.

Julius thanked Charon, and they all made their way to their ship and the long journey home. They were about to cast off when a voice called out to them to wait.

The figure ran along the creaking boards of the dock and toward the gangplank. But Julius's heart sank as he realized it wasn't Brutus at all.

"Felix, you bonehead!" cried Julius angrily. "Can't you forget about your ridiculous rock collection for one minute?"

Felix hopped on board and looked offended. "I wasn't collecting rocks!"

The sail was hoisted, and what little wind there was propelled them back toward the river Styx.

But Lucia wasn't having any of it! "This is RIDICULOUS!" she shouted. "We can't just leave Brutus there!" She leaped up and wrested the tiller from Julius's hooves. "Come on, Julius. Forget all that doom-and-gloom hokeypokey nonsense from Charon," she said defiantly. "We're going back for your brother, and NO ONE is going to stop us!"

"Are we even ALLOWED to do this?" wailed Felix. "Won't Sharon be mad at us?"

"I think that's the least of our troubles," muttered Cornelius, nervously eyeing the brewing storm clouds overhead.

As they reached the shore, Lucia vaulted into the water and ran toward the path.

Julius and the others jumped off the boat and swam ashore. "I've got a really bad feeling about this," whispered Cornelius. "We need to stop her!"

But it was too late. Just as Lucia reached the gate, a great booming voice rumbled through the air.

The ground shook so hard that everyone fell over.

The deep voice roared in anger. "WHO DARES ESCAPE MY DOMINION, THEN SEEKS TO PASS BACK THROUGH THE GATES A SECOND TIME?"

Lucia ran back to her friends, who all lay quivering on the ground.

"Where is that voice even coming from?" asked Felix.

Cornelius shakily pointed to the sky. "Th-th-there!" he stammered.

"That must be Hades himself!" replied Cornelius. "God of the underworld."

"Hades, god of Hades?" said Julius. "That's not confusing at all."

"When I get home," Felix said, laughing, "I'm going to be Felix, lord of Felix!"

"SILENCE!" bellowed Hades. "YOU ARE THE ONES WHO DARE RUN IN AND OUT OF MY WORLD, WILLY-NILLY!"

YOU SHALL ALL BURN IN THE FIERY RIVER OF ACHERON FOR THIS OUTRAGE!

The giant god held his staff high in the air, then brought it crashing down to the ground. There was a great flash and suddenly the animals found themselves in a metal cage suspended in midair.

"NO MERE MORTAL DARES ENTER THE UNDERWORLD TWICE AND LIVES TO TELL THE TALE!" boomed Hades. "FOR THIS CRIME, I SHALL CAST YOU INTO THE PITS OF HELL FOR ALL ETERNITY!"

As Hades held up his staff, ready to execute his judgment, Julius squeezed his hooves out of the cage to catch the god's attention. "WAIT! WAIT!" he cried, waving his arms. "We might be mortal, but this is all the fault of an IMMORTAL like yourself!"

Hades paused for a few seconds, then lowered his staff very slowly.

"SPEAK QUICKLY, HORSE-CREATURE. MY PATIENCE WEARS THIN."

"It was Heracles," cried Julius. "He made us do it!"

"HERACLES?" Hades gasped. "I SHOULD HAVE KNOWN!"

He made us do one of his labors.

Find a golden apple!

"LABORS?" asked Hades, slightly confused. "HE FINISHED HIS LABORS EONS AGO. WHAT IS HE UP TO NOW?"

He again raised his staff high in the air and brought it thundering to the ground. A great flash of lightning lit the sky as the ground trembled. Everybody screamed, expecting to be cast into the pits of hell. But much to their relief, they still hung in the air in their cage.

From below, a familiar figure appeared before them.

"That's him!" shouted Julius. "He made us look for a golden apple! He said his dad, Zoots, needed it!"

"How dare you!" replied Heracles. "I WAS looking for it, or I was about to, once I rested my bad knee." He waggled his leg for everyone to see. "Look, I twisted it escaping from that terror, Talos!"

"Yes, we found it, no thanks to you!" huffed Julius.

"Then you must give it to me at once!" cried Heracles, reaching desperately toward the cage. "I need it immediately!"

"Well, you're out of luck." Julius snorted. "Thanks to your wild goose chase, we lost my brother to the underworld."

Heracles looked remorseful. "I am truly sorry," he said. "Your brother was a fine zebra."

"Well, let's not get carried away," mumbled Milus.

"So we gave the apple to Sharon!" said Julius.

"Who?" gasped an enraged Heracles.

"HERACLES, THIS IS NOT THE FIRST TIME YOU HAVE STOOD BEFORE ME ACCUSED OF TREACHERY AND DECEIT!"

"But, Uncle, it wasn't like that, I swear!" pleaded Heracles.

"SILENCE!" roared Hades. "YOU HAVE BEEN WARNED MANY TIMES REGARDING YOUR HABIT OF RUNNING UP DEBTS AND DIRECTING OTHERS TO FIND TREASURES TO PAY YOUR BILLS."

"YOU CANNOT BE ALLOWED TO CONTINUE YOUR ANTICS, SO I HAVE DEVISED A PLAN TO KEEP YOU OCCUPIED," he continued.

"I HAPPEN TO KNOW OF A SECOND LABOR THAT YOU LEFT INCOMPLETE."

"NO, HALF-WIT, YOU MUST CLEAN THE AUGEAN STABLES!"

Back in the cage, Julius turned to Cornelius. "Cleaning stables? That's not much of a punishment!"

Cornelius let out a little chuckle. "These stables are different," he replied. "They're cursed with a never-ending supply of poop!"

"Oh, sweet!" Julius laughed.

In the distance, another great flash of lightning crackled across the sky. Heracles was gone.

Hades turned to Julius and his friends once more.

"THE CHARLATAN HAS GONE," said Hades, "AND, AS HIS UNCLE, I APOLOGIZE FOR HIS WRONGS."

"Losing my brother sure is some 'wrong.'" Julius sighed. Hades solemnly waved his staff, and the animals found themselves free of the cage and back on the ground.

Hey, your nephew promised us immortality if we found that apple!

"DID HE, NOW?" replied Hades. He pondered the antelope's words for a while. "BY ALL ACCOUNTS, YOU HAVE BEEN BRAVE IN THE FACE OF ADVERSITY AND CUNNING IN

YOUR ACCOMPLISHMENTS. I CANNOT OFFER YOU IMMORTALITY, BUT I CAN OFFER YOU A REWARD. EACH OF YOU THINK OF ONE THING THAT YOUR HEART DESIRES, AND IT WILL BE YOURS. THIS IS MY GIFT TO YOU AS RECOMPENSE FOR MY NEPHEW'S TRICKERY."

Hades raised his staff and brought it crashing back down to the ground with a flash.

In that instant, Julius and his friends found themselves back home by the lake.

Lucia ran up to Julius, who didn't seem to have a gift of any kind. "Julius!" she said. "What about you? What was your wish?"

Julius pointed to the nearby ridge.

"There!" he said. "That's my gift."

"I'm not sure I'd call bringing that idiot back to life a gift," growled Milus.

Ignoring the lion, Julius gave his brother a big hug. "You might be an idiot," he said. "But you're MY idiot!"

"I'm glad we're all back together again." Julius sighed, sitting down on the grass by the lake. "But after all that craziness, it would've been nice to have something to show for it."

"We didn't even get to keep that stupid golden apple," lamented Cornelius.

"Well," Felix said, "that's not entirely true."

Julius nearly fell into the lake with shock. "How on EARTH?"

"I swapped it for my golden banana," replied Felix. "He was very accommodating."

Cornelius burst into laughter. "You gave Charon, the ferryman to the gates of hell, a golden banana?" he cried. "That is amazing! I have a new respect for you, Felix."

"Maybe now we can all afford to open fancy spas!" Julius said with a laugh.

🌿 EPILOGUE 🌿

Hadrian sat at his desk admiring the soft, brightly patterned silk he'd been presented as a gift on his latest visit to his empire's eastern borders.

A guard suddenly entered the room and saluted his emperor.

"Ave, Caesar!" barked the guard.

"Yes, yes," Hadrian said with a huff. "What is it? Can't you see I'm busy?"

"No, I believe they're some kind of mythical dragon," mused Hadrian. "Its true symbolism is still unknown to us . . ." He quickly rolled the silk up and stuffed it into a desk drawer. "Not that it's any of YOUR business, soldier!" he blustered, suddenly realizing the guard's intrusion. "Now, tell me your news, or you'll find yourself wrestling lions in the Colosseum!"

The soldier stood up straight and coughed nervously. "Ahem . . . a Phrygian king seeks your counsel at once, O Caesar."

Hadrian stood up impatiently. "A Phrygian king?" he scoffed. "I don't have time to chat idly with Phrygian kings!"

Hadrian took a step back. "King Midas . . . to what do we owe the pleasure?" He went to put out his hand to greet the king, then recoiled almost immediately.

"I'M WEARING MY GLOVES!" yelled Midas.

"Yes, of course," replied Hadrian, and the men shook hands.

"Though perhaps I ought to disregard such formalities," huffed Midas, "seeing as Rome deems it necessary to send its greatest champion to STEAL from me and no doubt to OVERTHROW me, if my soldiers hadn't intervened in time."

"Greatest champion . . . ?" repeated Hadrian. "I don't understand."

"The ZEBRA!" roared King Midas. "If it is a war you want on your eastern frontiers, then it's a WAR you'll get!"

Hadrian slumped onto his chair and rubbed his chin. "The zebra. Of course." He sighed, exasperated. "No, it's not a war I want, Midas. But I do want to get rid of that blasted creature once and for all."

He pulled the exotic silk from his drawer and rubbed it softly. "And I think I have just the plan . . ."

TO BE CONTINUED . . .

🌿 ROMAN NUMERALS 🌿

Hello, readers! Julius has asked me and Felix to help explain the strange page numbers used throughout this book.

Instead of page numbers like 1, 2, and 3, you'll find I, V, X, and various other letters, which are Roman numerals—just like the Romans used for counting!

Even an idiot like me can understand them. Hooray!

Here are the seven letters that represent all the Roman numerals.

I = 1
V = 5
X = 10
L = 50
C = 100
D = 500
M = 1000

Thankfully, you won't find the last two. This book is big enough as it is!

Mostly, you simply add Roman numerals together to make different numbers:
II (1 + 1) = 2
VIII (5 +1+1+1) = 8
CLI (100 + 50 + 1) = 151

That seems easy enough! I'm off to collect some rocks.

CORNELIUS EXPLAINS THE COSMOS!

DRESS UP JULIUS AS AN ANCIENT GREEK HOPLITE!

1. Photocopy or trace the images on this page of Julius and the different parts of the Hoplite uniform.

2. Then glue the images onto thin sheets of cardboard.

3. Cut around each of the shapes, as shown, and color them in.

4. Now you can dress up Julius as an ancient Greek soldier by folding the small white tabs of the uniform carefully around his body.

1.

2.

3.

Assemble Julius's stand like this!

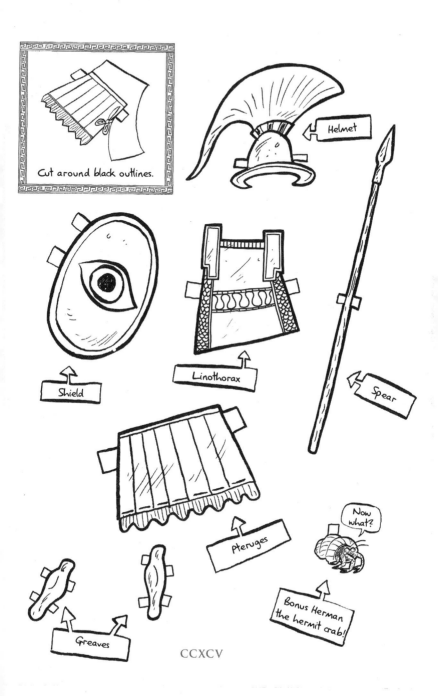

BE IMMORTALIZED ON YOUR OWN GREEK JUG OR URN!

1. Strike a dramatic pose.

2. Get a friend to draw you on a jug.

🌾 GLOSSARY 🌾

CERBERUS: The three-headed dog that guarded the gate to the underworld, stopping the dead from leaving and the living from entering. Once kidnapped by Heracles as one of his labors, Cerberus is sometimes depicted with fifty heads and a serpent's tail. Known to enjoy the dulcet tones of a lyre. The rasping caterwauling of a zebra, not so much.

CHARON: The ferryman of the dead who carried souls across the river Styx in exchange for a coin. His name is pronounced more like "Karen" than "Sharon," but let's not let solid facts spoil the fun. Pluto's largest moon is named after him.

GOLDEN APPLE: A fruit of Greek legend. It was said that anyone who ate a golden apple would never experience hunger, thirst, or illness ever again. Coveted by both gods and mortals, it was probably not an apple as we know it, but a quince, another fruit native to the Middle East and brought back to Greece by the army.

HADES: One of three brothers (the other two being Zeus and Poseidon) who defeated their father, Chronos, and the gods known as Titans, to claim the cosmos for themselves. They proceeded to divide the cosmos: Zeus got the skies, Poseidon the sea, and Hades, much to his annoyance, the underworld. To everyone's confusion, the underworld itself became known as Hades, and the Romans changed the god Hades's name to Pluto. (They also renamed Zeus Mickey Mouse, but it never really stuck.)

HERACLES: A demigod. The son of Zeus and Alcmene (a mortal), he possessed great strength, wit, and courage. He is most famous for completing twelve labors as a penance for a terrible crime—murdering his wife and children after being driven temporarily insane by the jealous goddess Hera. He was a great adventurer and enjoyed playing games; one of his favorites was beating up lions.

HESPERIDES: Goddess-nymphs entrusted to guard the golden apple tree. Gaia (the goddess of Mother Earth) gave the tree to the goddess Hera as a wedding gift when she married Zeus. The nymphs and their glowing apples were celebrated as the source of the golden light of sunset.

HOPLITES: Soldiers who formed the backbone of the Greek army. They carried large round shields and long spears. In battle, they would line up with their shields touching and their spears poking over the top in a formation known as a phalanx. Seeing a wall of shields and spears marching together in formation was enough to make anyone quake.

KING MIDAS: An ancient king of Phrygia who, after helping the god Dionysus, asked that everything he touched would turn to gold. This was great until he tried to eat anything . . . or tried to hug his daughter! He begged for the gift to be taken back. Dionysus agreed, and Midas was instructed to wash his hands in the river Pactolus. Legend has it that that's why the sand in the river Pactolus is so golden to this day.

LABYRINTH: An elaborate and confusing maze. It was designed and built by the legendary architect Daedalus for King Minos of Crete in order to hold the Minotaur captive. Daedalus made the labyrinth so complex, he could barely escape it himself! And when he finally did, Minos immediately imprisoned him and his son Icarus in order to preserve the labyrinth's secrets. But super-inventor Daedalus promptly made wings formed of feathers and wax, and he and Icarus flew to freedom. Unfortunately, Icarus got a bit cocky and flew too close to the sun. His wax wings melted, and . . . well, you can figure out the rest. There's a lesson in there somewhere!

LYRE: A stringed musical instrument played by the ancient Greeks. The god Apollo was considered a real virtuoso, and he taught Orpheus to become the best of mortal musicians. Orpheus then used his lyre to sing his way into the underworld on his journey to rescue his wife, Eurydice, from Hades.

MINOTAUR: A monster with the head of a bull and the body of a man (or the head of a man, with the body of a bull, depending on whom you listen to!). He was kept prisoner in the labyrinth by King Minos of Crete and regularly fed seven maidens and seven Athenian youths. Until, that is, the hero Theseus sneaked in and killed him. Theseus escaped the labyrinth by retracing his steps using string given to him by Minos's daughter, Ariadne. Quite simple when you think of it!

MOUNT OLYMPUS: Home to the pantheon of twelve Olympian gods (Zeus, Hera, Poseidon, Demeter, Athena, Hephaestus, Ares, Aphrodite, Apollo, Artemis, Hermes, and Dionysus). High above the clouds and out of sight of mere mortals, here the gods ate, drank, and argued like all normal families do, except the fate of the world lay in their hands. One god not invited up to Olympus was Hades, god of the underworld. He'd have said no if they asked him, anyway. Why would he want to sit on top of a stupid mountain, when he had an amazing vista of poisonous lakes and desolate fields filled with the roaming dead to look at?

NYMPHS: Nature goddesses, they ranked below the gods but were still summoned to attend assemblies on Mount Olympus. The nymphs controlled different aspects of nature—springs, clouds, trees, meadows, and more—and cared for plants and animals. Different from other goddesses, nymphs are usually depicted as beautiful young maidens who love to dance and sing.

THE ODYSSEY: One of the oldest and greatest stories in Western history, composed by the poet Homer. It tells the story of Odysseus, king of Ithaca, and his ten-year epic journey home from the Trojan War. He fought cyclops, six-headed monsters, and even ghosts. In fact, *The Odyssey* places only second in exciting Greek adventure stories—after *Julius Zebra: Grapple with the Greeks!*

OLYMPIC GAMES: Part of a religious celebration in honor of Zeus held in Olympia. At the first games, in 776 BCE, there was only one race, the stadion. This 600-foot-long running race was won by Koroibos, a cook. According to some traditions, the stadion was the only race at the games for the first thirteen festivals, until they decided it might be fun to do something else! The games are thought to have inspired the modern Olympic Games, begun in 1896.

RIVER STYX: The river that separated the world of the living from the world of the dead. The ancient Greeks believed its waters were deadly poisonous and would dissolve any container they were held in, except one made from the hoof of a horse or a donkey (or a zebra?).

TALOS: A bronze giant who guarded Crete. He was tasked with patrolling the island and circled it three times each day, throwing stones at the ships of unwanted visitors. His one weakness was his ankle, where a bronze nail was the only thing keeping his blood in place. That and getting rusty in the rain, obviously.

TROJAN HORSE: A mightily suspicious giant wooden horse. After ten years of fighting in the Trojan War, the Greek army pretended to sail away from the city of Troy, leaving only the wooden horse behind. Never ones to refuse a present, the Trojans dragged the enormous horse inside the city. When night fell, some of the Greeks—who had been hiding in the hollow belly of the horse the entire time—jumped out, opened the city gates, and let the rest of the Greek army in to rampage through Troy.

ZEUS: King of the Olympian gods. He sat on his throne atop Mount Olympus, dispensing wisdom and punishments. He was also stronger than all the other gods put together and had the ability to throw lightning bolts and control the weather.